SAVING HOUDINI

SAVING HOUDINI

MICHAEL REDHILL

DISCARDED

HarperCollins*PublishersLtd*

Saving Houdini
Copyright © 2014 by Michael Redhill.

Published by HarperCollins Publishers Ltd

First Canadian edition

HarperCollins books may be purchased for educational, business
or sales promotional use through our Special Markets Department.

HarperCollins Publishers Ltd
2 Bloor Street East, 20th Floor
Toronto, Ontario, Canada
M4W 1A8

www.harpercollins.ca

Library and Archives Canada Cataloguing in Publication
information is available upon request.

ISBN 978-1-44340-994-0

Printed and bound in the United States of America
RRD 9 8 7 6 5 4 3 2

There is nothing on this earth more to be prized than true friendship.

— THOMAS AQUINAS

For Benjamin and Maxime, brothers

The Globe and Mail

ADVERTISEMENT

Monday, September 5, 2011

THAT GREAT MYSTIFIER
BLOOM THE BEGUILER

**Begs the attention of his fellow
Torontonians**

As the abovementioned
ENTERTAINER

**— he of the nation's
greatest magical family —
WILL MAKE HIS REGULAR
QUINQUENNIAL TORONTO APPEARANCE**

**THIS OCTOBER 31, 2011
AT THE CANON THEATRE 8PM, SHARP**

WHEREIN HE WILL MARK
THE 85TH ANNIVERSARY
OF HARRY HOUDINI'S DEATH

1

Not me, not me, not me—

Dashiel Frederic Woolf sat completely still. He didn't look up but he knew they were near. They were coming. Closer and closer. His breath came jagged; his hands clenched into fists in his lap. There was a straining in the air, like a high note.

Not me, not me. Like a chant in his head. He couldn't help himself: he looked up. And someone was standing right beside him. A woman. She wore a satiny black and red dress. And she was pointing directly at him. The Alluring Katie. Just fifteen minutes ago, she'd been sawn in half. Too bad they'd put her back together.

"I think she means you, sweetheart," his mother said.

"I didn't put my hand up!" he growled at his mother. "I'm not going onstage!"

The audience was enthusiastic—three thousand people clapping in unison. "I think they want you to get up, Dash," his dad said. "You'll be great!"

"I'm gonna barf!"

"Well, make it spectacular, then," he said. "Get the whole front row."

Dashiel Woolf stood up. The audience went mad. This is a nightmare, he thought.

An hour earlier, he'd been stuffing wine gums into his mouth without a care in the world. He and his parents had been wandering around the lobby, watching the other theatregoers, reading the names on the signed photographs on the wall. Wine gums were kind of old-timey candies, but they lasted a long time and they came in all these colours. They were chewy too—but not *too* chewy—and the colours actually had different flavours. And unlike chocolate, they didn't melt in your mouth right away. You had to *work* a wine gum.

He'd been gnawing a purple one when a voice came over the sound system.

"Three minutes to curtain."

He looked down at his palm. There were five wine gums left and his mum had told him not to take anything sticky into the theatre. She'd also chosen the supposedly "handsome" suit he was wearing. He felt like he was in one of those boring black and white movies.

"Dash?" said his father with a horrified look on his face. "How many of those did you just put in your mouth?"

"*Fwoo?*" He'd jammed four of the remaining wine gums in.

"I don't even know why you like those things. They're not authentic, you know."

"Come on, we're going in," said his mother.

Thank god. His father was about to make a speech about how much better things had been in the past.

The second half of the show was going to be even awesomer than the first. And Bloom was going to do the Soap Bubble Vanish as a big finale. Dash tucked three of the wine gums behind his back teeth.

"They're more like gummy bears," his father was saying as they went down the aisle to their seats. "The original Maynards wine gums are sort of leathery. More like jerky than candy. There's a dusty feeling when you put them in your mouth."

"Uh-huh," Dash said, his voice hollowed out by a cheekful of candy.

"You look like a squirrel," said his father.

"You look old."

"You smell funny," said his father, grinning.

The lights were flashing and everyone moved into their seats. A round, white spot hung in the middle of the red curtain, like a full moon. His mum draped her arm over his shoulder.

"In a year's time," she whispered into his ear, "you're going to be a teenager and I'm not going to have to lean over to put my arm around you."

*

Each time the magician Joseph Bloom was scheduled to come back to Toronto, tickets would go on sale a year in advance and sell out in less than ten minutes. He toured the world with his show, but he made a point of returning once every five years to his hometown. He'd always do something special for his quinquennial. "Something to keep you another five years," he'd always say. Somehow, last year, Dash's mother had snagged four tickets.

The fourth ticket had been for Dash's best friend Alex, but Alex had moved away in the summer to Holland. Dash hadn't even known where Holland was, never mind that there was a town in it called *Leiden*. His mum kept bugging him to invite someone else, but what would have been the point? Alex was gone now, and it was Alex's ticket and no one was going to replace him. They were good tickets too: right on the aisle. Too bad for Alex. He could have stayed in Toronto with his dad instead of moving away with his mum, could have kept going to the same school, and then he'd be here now, in the third row, for the most famous magic trick on the planet.

His loss.

Dash had insisted that the aisle seat be left empty.

He and his parents moved into their own seats just as the auditorium lights faded. He watched the audience settle around him. He finally chewed the purple wine gum. *That's* how grapes should taste, he thought.

"Ladies and gentlemen," bugled a voice, as the moon on the curtain lost the last of its lustre. "Please welcome back to the Canon Theatre stage . . . Joseph Bloom: *Bloom the Beguiler!*"

In the olden days, there had been the great *H*s like Houdini and Howard Thurston, but to Dash, the *B*s had always been the Best. B for *Bloom*. The beguiling Bloom. And *B* was also for Bloom the Incomparable—the Beguiler's father, who had once eaten a pincushion full of needles and then pulled them out of his mouth with a magnet. And then there was Blumenthal the Believer, Bloom's grandfather. They were one of the most famous magic families of all time, and Bloom still did some of his grandfather's tricks. Blumenthal's signature opening had been to produce a rose from the inside of an empty fist. It would grow out of his hand, thorns and all, to a foot in height.

It had been the grandfather who'd invented the Soap Bubble Vanish. He'd only performed it once, in 1926, and although the trick had made him briefly famous, he retired it, and afterward, according to legend, he wouldn't speak of it. When he passed away, the secret died with him, and the apparatus was lost.

But somehow, Bloom was doing it tonight. How the trick had come into his possession was a mystery. He would only say that he was doing it in honour of his grandfather and to mark the death of Harry Houdini, who had died on Halloween eighty-five years ago this very evening.

Dash watched the second half of the show in a sort of blissed-out trance. Bloom performed The Flying Fish—a terrifying escape. Then a rope trick in which a small length of rope was stretched and thickened until it reached across the stage. Then The Living Marionette, a classic invented by Bloom's father, and She's Beside Herself, in which the Alluring Katie was separated—while standing upright—into two pieces, with the doors to the boxes open the entire time. After a trick with shadows and swords, the stage went dark, and a sharp circle of light appeared on the back wall.

A steel ring rolled out all by itself from the wings and spun to a stop in the middle of the stage.

It was time for the grand finale.

Bloom walked slowly, regally, to the middle of the stage and stood there before them with a little metal wand in his hand. He had changed into a plain grey suit with a silver tie. He picked the ring off the stage and *ting*ed all around the inside of it with the metal wand, and the sound of the steel chimed out over them all.

"The circle of life," he began now, holding the ring out to the audience. Flat on, it looked like a washer the size of a manhole. There was a groove in its surface that made a perfect circle within the ring. "This greatest mystery of all. How we get here, where we go. What life *is*, what forces govern it. I would like to demonstrate to you how deep a mystery it really is. I must warn you, though: this trick is not for the faint-hearted. I save it for last because I suspect you will need time to recover. But in order to do it, I'm going to need a volunteer for . . . the *Soap Bubble Vanish*."

A forest of hands shot upwards in the auditorium and instantly the room was acrackle with energy. Dash, his heart pounding, kept his hands tightly in his lap. He was going to be one of only a handful of people ever to see this trick performed. And he had a third-row seat!

The lights came up, and Bloom's three assistants began walking the aisles on either side, looking left and right, searching for a volunteer.

2

The Alluring Katie held her hand out to him.

He had no choice. He groaned under his breath and rose, and the applause thickened. Then he was in the aisle and walking to the stage.

Katie helped Dash up the steps to where Bloom was standing. Bloom the Beguiler. *In person.*

"You look like you're being marched to your execution," Bloom said, and the audience laughed.

Dash wiped the cold sweat off his forehead with the back of his hand. His heart was breakdancing.

"What is your name, young man?"

"Dashiel," he muttered.

"What is that?"

"DASHIEL," he said louder, and he heard his voice thrown around the auditorium.

"Well, young man, tell me . . ." Bloom paused, admiring his volunteer. "Have we met before?"

"Only in a couple of books I've read."

"Oh, so you know *about* me? You know what I can *do* . . ."
Bloom lifted the ring and looked at Dash through it. Now the audience's laughter turned nervous. "Are you not a little worried?"

"I'm *very* worried," Dash said.

The magician turned to the audience looking like he was holding back a laugh. "I see our young friend has done his homework! I assure you, Master Dash, you have no reason to worry. But then again, worry is not a rational thing, is it? Magic is irrational. Maybe you *should* be worried!" He looked out at the audience again and gave them a clownish wink. They roared with laughter. "I can always ask someone else to come up here . . ."

"No," said Dash. He wasn't going to chicken out in front of thousands of people. "I'll do it."

Bloom clapped him on the shoulder and squeezed. "Brilliant! Now, let's have a look at you." He pretended to dust Dash off. "Are you going to be vanished with your tie all a mess like that?"

"I . . ."

"Now, now," Bloom said, "let's look our best for the people. Will someone please fix this poor boy's tie?"

He gently urged Dash toward the wings, and Dash walked off in a daze, blinded by the light. A flutter of laughter came his way. He could taste lime wine gum at the back of his throat. In the darkness of the wings, a pair of hands reached out to him and began fiddling with his tie.

"There's a chalk ring on the stage," a boy's voice whispered.

"Put the steel ring on it, okay? Or you might get bonked with something."

Dash's eyes began to adjust and he saw a kid about his age standing in front of him. The boy had a muss of black hair on his head and no clue how to fix a tie. The footlights picked out his blue eyes.

"Your name's Dash?"

"Yeah."

"Well, someone left this for you," the boy said, and he slid a small, white envelope into Dash's breast pocket. Then, before Dash had a chance to say anything, the boy shoved him back onstage.

"Oh," said Bloom, seeing the state of his tie now. "We'll have to fire the wardrobe people, I guess!" Dash glanced back into the wings, but the kid was gone. "Young man," said Bloom, "will you take this ring from me and place it somewhere on the stage? Anywhere you like."

Dash took the ring. It wasn't very heavy, but it was solid. He walked back a few steps. There was a faint chalk circle exactly the circumference of the ring, just as the boy had said. Dash pretended to hesitate, looking around, and Bloom watched him, a tiny flicker of a smile playing at the corner of his mouth. Then Dash put the ring down exactly on its mark.

"Now, if you will, take your position *inside* that iron ring." Dash stepped into it carefully. "Anything unusual?"

"Um, everything?"

The audience laughed.

"Stomp on the floor there. Solid, isn't it? No trap door?" Dash shook his head. "And now open your arms to show there are no unseen wires anywhere around you."

Dash spread his arms wide and turned in a slow circle. The room revolved in front of him: the audience, the theatre boxes along the wall ranging upwards like steps. Then the bare backstage, the light intensifying on it. Bloom . . . and all those spectators' eyes.

"Let us continue," Bloom said. He gestured into the fly space above and something began to move downwards. A second ring appeared, lowering on cables. It seemed heavier than the first, and Bloom guided it so it didn't hit Dash on the head as it passed around his body to the floor. The upper ring made a smart clacking noise as it came into contact with the lower.

"Are you ready?"

"I guess so."

"Do you know what is going to happen, young Dashiel?"

"No . . ."

"Do you want to hear the truth?" Bloom leaned in and whispered, loudly enough for the audience to hear, "I don't either! But . . . that is no reason not to find out!"

He stepped back, lifting his hands. The cables began to draw the ring back up over Dash's body. As they did, a luminous, undulating film rose with the ring. When the film reached the level of his chest, Dash could smell it: it was acrid and soapy. Something in the smell settled his stomach a little, and as the chill of the bubble cooled his face and chest, he felt a calm envelop him. Finally, the ring passed over his head and Dash was looking at the audience through a wavering, impossibly thin, slightly blue screen. It made the faces in front of him sway and shrink and bulge. There were his parents, sitting in the third row, giving him a thumbs-up. Dorks.

And then he was feeling oddly sleepy . . . He watched Bloom approach him with a long, polished needle in his hand. The light was bursting everywhere. He listened to Bloom's voice:

"The line that divides life from death is as thin as the bubble that encases young Dashiel tonight. But only in magic can you vanish and . . . COME BACK!"

The tip of Bloom's pin touched the soapy membrane of the bubble and colour rushed toward it like something flowing into a hole. The lights were strange and slow, and Dash saw his parents' faces moving away from him. The balcony at the back of the house, a dirty colour now in the shifting light, was spreading wide and thin like taffy. Then it was like he'd just taken off on an airplane and a great rushing sound filled his ears. There was a sudden, hollow *pop*, so big he felt it in his bones.

Then there was nothing. Emptiness above him and below him. He was floating in silence. At some point he had closed his eyes. He felt he could be rising, but then he was falling, slowly, and the stage floor came up to meet his feet. He could hear himself breathing in the hollow silence. It was *really* quiet.

Too quiet.

He opened his right eye half a squint. Through his lashes, he saw seats in the theatre. But they were empty. Rows and rows of empty seats.

He closed the eye. *Okay. Yep. That's* not right.

Maybe there was another theatre in the basement of the Canon. Or he'd spun around a hidden wall into another auditorium. Except he was pretty sure there was only one in this theatre. And this one was identical in every way to the one he'd been watching the show in. It also looked . . .

Newer.

He opened both eyes. It was the same place, all right, but Bloom, his assistants, the audience, and even the ring he had been standing in were gone.

Dash leaned over and barfed.

3

"HEY!" came an angry voice.

Dash stood fixed to his spot, rib cage shuddering with fear.

"Hey!" shouted the voice. "Whadya think you're doin' up there? How didya get in here anyhow?"

A man wearing a tight black suit and a messy black beard came down the aisle. He didn't look at all friendly. "You kids coming in here at night these days? Is that what this is? Eh? You kids squeakin' in through the fence in the parkin' lot?"

"I don't know what you mean—"

The man climbed the stairs at the side of the stage, waggling a long flashlight. He shone its hard, white light into Dash's eyes.

"EH! Whadya do to my stage! You know what one a' these feels like on the backa yer leg?"

"My parents were just here, sir. I, I was—"

"MARCH! Get your person offa my stage before I leave an imprint on it! By which I mean your PERSON." He slapped the barrel of the flashlight against his palm.

Dash found his legs and backed away to the edge of the stage. No adult had ever threatened to hit him. Some other kids, maybe, but not adults, and this guy was *for real*. Dash jumped down from the front of the stage and turned around.

"Does your boss know you threaten kids?"

The man's face went white with rage. He started clomping down the stairs after Dash. "My boss? You wanna talk to my boss? You're talkin' to'm right now!"

What in the world was going on? Where were his parents? How did they get everyone out of the theatre so quickly? Dash ran up the aisle to the doors and pushed through them into the lobby—

And stopped in his tracks.

It was different out here. Totally different. The carpeting had changed colour from red to blue, and the concession stand was now on the right. Had he come out another door? He speed-walked over to the candy counter. There was a pack of Maynards under the glass, but it was packaged differently. And beside the wine gums was a package of candy called Adams Black Jack Sucking Candy. He hadn't seen that during the intermission. Nor had there been any Fox's Glacier Mints—"In a BOTTLE," it said on the label. Since when did they start putting mints into *bottles*?

He was so stunned he could do nothing but turn and stare as the theatre owner came bounding into the lobby, the auditorium doors banging back against the walls.

"Hold on! Just wait!" Dash said, his hands up. "Let me say something!"

"You have two and a half seconds."

"Is this—?"

"Time's up!"

"Wait! Hold on! Is this the Canon Theatre?"

"What cannon theatre?" the man snarled.

Dash backed up quickly through the concourse. The doors to the street were still a floor down. He made a run for it, taking the marble steps two at a time. He heard the echo of his pounding footfalls along the tiled hall as he raced to the exits. He rattled a door: locked. He tried the rest of them quickly in succession. Locked. Locked. Locked.

On the other side of the glass, it was peacefully snowing. Dash stared. Something was very wrong with that scene.

He heard the man's slow, confident step behind him. Dash turned and pressed his back against the doors. The man waggled a ring of keys at him as he crossed in front of Dash and opened a steel case on the wall: a telephone box. He smiled with malicious triumph as he dialled a number. Then, he hung up and crossed his arms over his chest.

"Shouldn't be long now," he said. He stared at Dash, enjoying his triumph. The door was cold against his back. Where were his parents? How was he going to get out of this?

The corners of the man's mouth twitched upwards and he raised his hand toward the doors. "Ah, they're always around when you need them."

Dash spun to see a pair of men with huge, fake-looking moustaches approaching the theatre.

The theatre owner grabbed his jacket collar and held Dash tightly against one glass door as he unlocked the other.

"Good evening, Officers," he said.

Those were police?

"Good evening," they replied as one.

"I think we have an escapee from the orphanage."

Dash was pinned inside the circle of men. They smelled like gasoline and leather. His eyes searched between them, frantic, hunting for a way out.

Beyond, in the street, he saw a big, black, cartoonish-looking car go trundling by. *What the . . .* "Where am I?" he yelled, pulling frantically in their clutches.

"That won't work on us," replied one of the moustaches. "Which home are you from, boyo?"

"Home? I'm from Toronto!"

"Oh, rah-rah," said the theatre owner. "He was making a mess on my stage!"

"I didn't mean to!"

"Come on now," said the other moustache.

As the policeman's hand stretched toward him, Dash felt a wave of energy flood his body and his heart began to race, like there was an engine behind his ribs. He pushed himself into one of the policemen and stomped on his foot, hard, hollering at the top of his lungs. The man instinctively shot back, shouting, and let go of Dash, and he made a pencil-dive between them, ramming the door open with his shoulder as he barrelled free.

He landed on the sidewalk with a thud, and felt the heavy glass door already closing on his leg. There was no time to think—he bounded up and lurched into the road. Those cartoon cars were everywhere, with their square hoods and huge wheels with wooden spokes.

He ran across the road, dodging the slow-moving vehicles. He heard whistles behind him rise in shrill discord.

On the other side, where the Eaton Centre was supposed to be—where *downtown* was supposed to be!—there were *houses*. Instead of a sparkling mall half a kilometre long, festooned with video screens and bright billboards, there were little red-brick houses with wooden gables. A man stood in a window on the second floor of one of those houses, holding a cat in his arm and smoking a pipe.

Dash crouched between a pair of parked cars stubbed up against the curb at an angle. Made it easier to hide, at least. He could hear angry voices nearby. He poked his head out and looked back at the theatre.

It *was* the Canon Theatre. At least it was the same building with the same little gargoyles on the front. But the sign on top of the marquee said THE PANTAGES, and on either side were houses and stone buildings faced with columns. He ducked down again and spied through the wheel-spokes as black, gleaming boots went by. They really wanted to catch him, and do whatever people did to an eleven-year-old trespasser here. Wherever *here* was.

He crouched between cars and tried to make himself as small as possible. No wonder Bloom's grandfather had only done the trick once! Did Bloom know he was going to send Dash into this bizarro world? Was it possible this was *how* the trick worked? He'd read about the black arts, but he didn't believe in wizards or sorcerers. This was just a magic trick! It had to be a trick!

It had to be.

He edged into traffic again, behind his pursuers. Almost all the cars had the word *Ford* stuck on their fronts in steel cursive. They weren't like any Fords *he'd* ever seen: they moved in fits and starts, bunched up, and sometimes there'd be a *parp-parp* noise when someone honked their horn. He kept moving. Another noise added itself now to this unreal, too-real world, a deafening blare in the distance that bloomed into a hundred trumpets being blown through the wrong ends—a fire truck. He had to leap aside to avoid being crushed by its giant tires. Five firemen rode standing up in the back.

"OI! You! Stop right there!"

Dash dropped into another gear, running, his legs churning like he was riding his dad's exercise bike on the hardest setting. The intersection in front of him was packed with people. Every last one of them, even the kids, was wearing a hat. He plunged into the crowd, his heart beating so hard it hurt. His lungs began to sting, his chest tightened. The air was freezing in his nose and mouth.

Ahead of him, a streetcar ground on its tracks toward the intersection. It was a grey train with doors at the front and back and a bunch of wooden window frames along its side. There were a lot of people gathered around its back door. Dash swivelled toward the roadway again, but now there were two more policemen running for him, shrieking on their whistles. *Oh god oh god oh god*—he was going to get caught. He heard a voice behind him.

"KID! Hey, kid!"

A man at the rear of the crowd waiting for the streetcar was holding his hand out to him, gesturing furiously.

"Come on! Hurry!"

Dash ran toward him. His legs were going to give out. The man parted the jostling crowd with his hand as a load of passengers descended onto the sidewalk. They were met with a rush of newsboys who closed in behind Dash, blocking the men with the whistles. The newsboys cried something like *Mailnempire!* and *Tyrannosaur, tyrannosaur, one penny!* There were five of them, none older than fourteen, and more stood on crates by the storefronts. One was smoking a cigarette!

"Hurry to the front there," said the man, pushing him forward. Like everyone else he wore a hat—a plain, grey felt hat, like from the old movies his parents loved—but he had his brim pulled down low over his eyes. "Go on, then," he said, and Dash whispered a hurried thank you as he passed him and jumped up into the streetcar.

The doors rolled shut and the streetcar began moving. Dash watched through the window as the red-faced policemen blew their whistles in frustration. Above them, two giant wooden billboards loomed over the street, lit up with spotlights against the dusk. The snow came down into the middle of it all, a million white pinpoints against the glow, like stars falling into the street. The newsboys in their suspenders and flat, tartan caps had already rushed the doors of the next streetcar.

Dash's legs quaked. He looked down the aisle: he was standing among . . . well, strangely dressed people. People who looked like they were going home to their suppers. Some of them reading the newspapers they'd just bought. Three of the ladies were knitting. And everyone's shoes looked so . . . *old-fashioned*. Even the new ones, the shiny ones, looked old.

Maybe he *had* hit his head? That would explain it. Fat lot of good the backstage kid's warning had been.

This was impossible. Maybe he'd lost his mind. But he was certain he wasn't dreaming, because you know the difference between real life and dreams when you're in real life. It feels a certain way: the weight of your own feet on the ground, the pressure of something in your hand.

And this all felt so *real*. The way the floor was bumping under his feet, the smell of cigarette smoke. (More than half the people on the car were puffing away.) But *how*?

The streetcar was already slowing, and a few people rose from their seats. One of them was the man who'd parted the crowd for him.

"Take my seat," he said. "You look like you could use a rest." He nodded kindly. He wore a dark, wool overcoat, and on its lapel there was a single, plain black ring like a brooch. No bigger than a ring you would wear on your finger. He stepped down and vanished into the shadows.

Dash sat down as the streetcar lurched forward again. He watched the road stretch away through the glass at the front. Where was he going? East. Toward his part of town. The part he lived in. Maybe he'd just stay on the streetcar until he recognized something.

Soon the streetlights of downtown were behind them. He turned and saw the intersection of Yonge and Dundas pulsing in the distance, an egg of light nested in a darkening sky. Dash realized he was sitting on a newspaper and he shifted to pluck it out. It was the *Toronto Star* (*oh*, he thought, *tyrannasaur*). He read the date.

Then he read it again.

Monday, October 18, 1926.

The headline declared: HAIR CUT FROM HEAD OF "MISS X" WAS FALSE SAYS "HOAX WOMAN."

He stood up and slapped the newspaper down on the seat again. He sat on it. *I'm going to freak out. Right now. Freak out on an antique streetcar full of antique people and they're gonna put me in handcuffs and dump me in an orphanage.* He pursed his mouth and made little puffing breaths, and then he barked "HA HA!" out loud in a panicked voice and had to look down at his feet, which seemed to be shuffling back and forth of their own accord. Nobody was noticing him lose it.

Just then, a man who'd been seated beside the driver rose and came down the streetcar collecting fares. He wore a cap, and a leather strap hung heavy over his shoulder. Dash shoved his hand into his pocket and found the change from his wine gums, as well as the wine gum he hadn't managed to stuff into his mouth. He watched other people pay. Two big brown coins. What the heck were those? He was going to have to get off. Who knew what they did to kids in 1926 who trespassed in theatres and jumped fares on streetcars?

Suddenly the streetcar stopped hard and he put his hand out to brace himself. Five or six people timbered forward into others. There was a bright light ahead in the road, and Dash smelled what it was over the cigarette fumes: fire. People were tugging down the windows and craning their necks out. Finally the driver opened the doors and asked everyone to step down. As Dash left the streetcar, he saw the fire truck he'd noticed earlier pumping thick ropes of water over a shed burning wildly in a muddy yard. Everyone seemed excited, and it was easy for Dash to separate from the riders and cross the street unseen.

They'd stopped at River Street. He knew where he was now: on the edge of the Don Valley. Down below ran great channels of concrete roadway and steel rail and a river. River Street's name had always made sense to him, not like Parliament, which didn't have a parliament, or Front Street, which wasn't at the front of anything. But he could really see the river now, as he left Dundas and the crowd. The river had actual *banks,* not highways, and reeds grew along its edges!

Beyond River Street and the valley was Dash's house. And he couldn't stay here. It was getting colder, and it was still snowing.

He'd left his coat at Bloom's magic show. He could see it there, in his mind's eye, draped over the back of his third-row seat: his nice, warm coat.

He'd go home. He'd just go to his house. He knew how to get there, and once he was there, maybe everything would be fine. Maybe the second he walked through the door of his house, he'd pop out on the Canon Theatre stage and everyone would start clapping. And then he'd get in the car with his parents and go home.

Maybe it would be that easy.

He walked back to Dundas. It felt like he was entering a lit-up diorama. The shed, still burning over in the muddy yard, was flickering as if under its own spotlight. The trees caught light in their lower branches from the lamps, and the whole town glittered tightly in the west.

He followed the road and crossed the footbridge over the river to the east end. He would be in his own neighbourhood in ten minutes. But if this was 1926—had his neighbourhood even been built yet? He came to a stop, shuddering. His guts churned. What if even his house was gone?

The old jail was up the hill, sitting alone. He passed it and went up Broadview Avenue. Broadview wasn't paved: the road was made of crushed stone. Another streetcar came along and rang its bell at him. He wasn't sure if it was a greeting or a warning. They didn't look too stable, those rattling tin boxes full of people smoking.

And now here was Victor Avenue. He was standing at the end of his own street.

He began to walk down it, in this dream that wasn't a dream.

4

The trees on Victor Avenue were smaller than he recalled, but there were more of them. Still, the street felt familiar. So familiar it made him dizzy, like he might have to sit down, or run off shouting at the top of his lungs. He decided to sit. There was a slab of stone at the curb in front of number 36. He slowly lowered himself onto its cold surface. As the natural light vanished, the little pole-mounted lanterns along the street buzzed to life.

Okay. So he'd been sent back in time. Whatevs. Everything was just as you would expect, *if* you'd been zapped back eighty-five years. There were houses and streets just like the houses and streets he knew. Except they were in 1926. No biggie, right? Someone would help him. Surely.

He got up and continued walking. He passed his friend Tim's house, and the house where the baby twins lived. On the other side of the street: that was Carl and Wendy's; Carl was a fireman. Then Louie Leonidis, who was ninety, probably, and wore his pants up to his rib cage. Dash liked Louie a lot. Louie was the first old man he'd ever really gotten to know. He was very concerned with his lawn. Or maybe he just liked to be outdoors.

Heh, Dashy! he would say, waving a spindly arm. He was an old Greek man with a small black moustache that was missing some hairs, or else they were very white. *You're a good boy, heh?*

I'm a lost boy!

He was almost at his house. Some things began to feel really different now. This part of Victor Avenue was quite overgrown with trees. There was one on almost every lawn. Many of the trees downtown had finished changing colours and were shedding their leaves, but here, the street was under a high tunnel of red and orange. Beyond them, down at the end of the street, there seemed to be *woods*.

Was he some kind of ghost now? Walking among the dead, before his own birth? Or was he the real and only him, the only Dashiel Woolf who'd ever existed, and now there was no him in the present?

As he was thinking this, he came to number 94. His house. He paused and swallowed. Then he walked along the flagstones to the steps and climbed them. There was something wrong about the house, he could feel it. He knocked, almost unwillingly, and heard the sound echoing. There were no drapes over the windows and it was dark inside. He looked through the window in the front door and saw empty rooms.

He tried the handle and the door floated open before him, onto an abandoned foyer with bare walls. There were shadowy discolourations where pictures had once hung.

"H-hello?"

He stepped in. His breath came out in little puffs of steam.

"Hello?"

There was no answer.

He crept down the front hall. It was his house, all right, but there was nothing and no one in it. He saw a sheet of paper lying on the floor in the living room, handwriting on it:

26. Long-stemmed glasses, pewter salt and pepper shakers

27. Candles, candleholders, baskets

28. Saucers and side plates

29. Tablecloths and napkins

It went on like that—a list of things someone had packed.

The house showed other signs of having been recently emptied. There were bits of newsprint scattered on the floor, and a tall stack of magazines stood forgotten in a corner. And little galaxies of dust swirled in the dim streetlight that came through the side window in the dining room.

A family had moved out. A new family had not yet arrived. It was eerie, like there were presences here, echoes. But he was the only one in the house.

He climbed the stairs as quietly as he could. None of the steps creaked—it must have taken years for the house to age and get the creaks he knew. These stairs were pretty new. They even smelled woody.

The second floor was as vacant as the downstairs. His parents' room, his room, the office where his father sometimes worked at night, were all in their correct positions, but silent and empty. His parents would not arrive here until 1995, after they married. A long time from now.

He retreated down the hall to his bedroom. He recognized the boards on his floor, their grain. The face in that one, the long letter *N* in another one. The black knotholes on two separate boards that, if he crossed his eyes just right, would merge into one. He stood beside the window and surveyed the space in bewilderment. His bed would be here. His bookshelf, here. His blue dresser across from the bed, and behind it, in the corner, the little painted bookshelf. Then the door to the closet, right where it had always been, would always be. He had a little hoop up on that door with a net in it. His mother was always begging him not to use the tennis ball. "Use the Nerf that came with it!" she'd call upstairs, and he'd call down, "The Nerf doesn't bounce right!" In his mind he could hear it bounce.

Breathe, he told himself again. Who knew it could be so hard to breathe?

He had to pee. He went down the hall to the bathroom. *That* was a toilet? The seat was made of wood! And there was a wooden box high up on the wall with a furry-looking rope hanging from it.

He peed for one whole minute. He peed so long he started laughing, but the sound in the empty house was strange and creepy. Dash rushed back to his bedroom and huddled under the window. He took off his suit jacket and covered himself with it for warmth. He tried to breathe normally.

Something was poking him in the chin. He felt around in his breast pocket and found the envelope the boy had tucked into it. He took it out and opened it.

There was a piece of newsprint inside, folded tightly. The paper had the feel of cloth and it was a deep dusty white, like the colour of old gravestones. Dash unfolded it carefully, worried it would tear, but it didn't.

It was the bottom half of a page from the *Montreal Gazette* dated Thursday, October 21, 1926. Three days later than the date on the newspaper he'd found in the streetcar. Why would that kid have given him an old piece of newsprint? It was numbered page 5 at the bottom on one side, 6 on the other. He could feel the letters imprinted onto the paper, like they'd been hammered into it.

There was an advertisement for the movie *Men of the Night*, starring someone named Herbert Rawlinson. The ad showed a man in a mask trying to open a safe. There was also an article about a child who had been struck and killed by a car downtown. The article called the child "ill-starred." There was an advertisement for Orange Crush, a drink Dash knew well, but he'd never seen it in a ribbed bottle like the one shown in the clipping. It looked like it came in a beehive. Below were the racing results from Blue Bonnets Raceway and the time of the day's sunrise and sunset. There was a torn-off story about some fight in the government about alcohol.

He turned the page over. On that side he found a headline: VISITING PROFESSOR HOUDINI CHALLENGES SPIRITUALISTS AT McGILL.

There was a picture—just the bottom half—showing a bunch of people in an audience. The photo had been taken from the side of the room. Men and women sat in folding wooden chairs, and many stood along the walls, crowding in. There were kids scattered in the back, holding hats in their hands. They had strange, smooth-combed short hair in 1926. Houdini's chest and legs were just below the tear, the bottom of a dark tie covered in white stars visible, his legs crossed neatly. Black socks and gleaming black shoes.

If the picture *had been* taken on October 20, then this would be one of the last images of Harry Houdini ever published. He died on Halloween 1926, in a hospital in Detroit, supposedly from the complications of appendicitis. Dash knew all about it. Anyone who cared about magic knew about the mystery of Harry Houdini's death.

In Montreal, someone had asked him if he could take a punch, but before the great magician was ready, the man struck him hard in the stomach. Earlier, Houdini's wife, Bess, had begged him to get a security guard. He'd become unpopular with swamis and mediums, who made good money by claiming they could communicate with the dead. Houdini had received threats after calling them vultures and charlatans. He said they preyed on people who were in mourning.

Some people believed the punch had ruptured his appendix; others thought he'd already been sick when he arrived in Montreal.

Whichever theory was right, one fact remained: he'd died. Ten days after the piece of newspaper Dash held in his hand had been printed.

His head swam. Why had he been given this? Was this supposed to help him? And if so, how?

He refolded the newspaper and tried to slip it back into its envelope, but it wouldn't go in all the way. There was something else in there. Dash pulled the clipping out and saw that there was also a small, white card. There was a message on it, a *typed* message. Dash had never seen actual typewriting before. It said:

```
IF YOU WOULD LIKE, PLEASE JOIN US TOMORROW
AT 4 O'CLOCK. 64 ARUNDEL AVENUE. THERE WILL
BE SNACKS AND LEMONADE.
```

He turned the card over. Blank. Whoever had sent this envelope didn't want him to know who they were. But why would someone invite him over without telling him who they were? *Very* creepy.

Dash slumped against his bedroom wall. None of this made any sense. He didn't *know* anyone in 1926, and no one knew him. Maybe it was a trap. If you were alone in the past and got into trouble, there wouldn't be anyone to help you or even miss you. They could do whatever they wanted to you.

If you would like. Strange thing to say. He got sent back almost a hundred years and the only thing anyone had to tell him wasn't all that urgent?

After a while, he moved to the middle of the room and stood there. He closed his eyes and again imagined the room as he knew it. Then he opened them and aimed his palm at the ceiling, feeling the weight of an invisible tennis ball in his hand. Hefting it once, twice, he launched it toward the basket. *Alley-oop. Tonk.* Off the door jamb and through the net. Then *pok pok pok* as the ball bounced back to him.

One more minute, Dash, then I want you to stop! His mother's voice.

The phantom ball moved in a graceful arc through the air and back to his hand. He let his arms fall to his sides and stared at the door to the empty closet, the house enveloping him in its strange silence. He lowered his head. He wouldn't have wanted you to know this, but he wept.

5

Dashiel Woolf had a pain in his belly that was like the blast radius of an exploding black hole. It was impossible to ignore. He needed food.

He'd woken up on the floor of his (future) bedroom, still in 1926, his suit jacket folded to make a pillow for his head. He looked out the window: it seemed to be mid-morning already. Amazing to think that even in the midst of a calamity, he could still sleep in.

He put his jacket on, stuffing his tie into the pocket. Every male person he'd seen on the streets of Toronto the previous evening had been wearing a suit jacket of some kind. Thank goodness his mother had forced him to put on a suit for Bloom's show! He couldn't imagine showing up here in a skateboarding T-shirt. But his own suit jacket was somewhat worse for wear after being slept on, and if he was going to be here for any length of time, he was going to have to get clothes that looked a little more like the strangely stiff-looking suits made of rough fabric worn here. And a pair of those crummy shoes too. His shoes were too good.

But clothing and food was going to take money, and he had none.

Wait. He had *some* food!

He dug into his pocket. The wine gum was still there. He pulled it out and picked the lint off it. It was an orange one. Orange was like orange *juice*. And it was, after all, breakfast time. He popped it into his mouth. It was still fresh! He heard his father in his head, comically chiding him: *Fresh? You could bury a pack of those until after the apocalypse then dig 'em up, and they'd be exactly the same.*

Ha. Good one, old man. That's what Dash would've said. *Good one.*

At this hour, his father would be mumbling as he tried to get out of bed. He wasn't a morning person. "It's genetic," he'd once said to Dash. "Runs on the male side. Embrace it." His father would be waking up just around the corner from where Dash was sitting right now.

That would be a morning in his *real life.* He didn't know what *this* was, but whatever it was, a single wine gum was not going to get him through it.

He went down the stairs into the echoing front hall and left the house. Standing on the sidewalk, he stared up. The brightly coloured tree canopy seemed to be holding the blue sky between red and orange palms. Victor Avenue was still empty.

He zigzagged along side streets to Danforth Avenue. There

were plenty of people on the main thoroughfare of the neighbourhood: men in delivery trucks that had Model T hoods with pickup beds in the back; men and ladies on bicycles; a policeman on a bicycle (Dash looked away, quickly but casually). On the corner, there was a "Loblaws Groceteria"—not the Loblaws his father shopped at, but a little storefront with two windows, one full of cans and boxes, the other with pyramids of apples, stacked loaves of bread in paper wrapping, and a side of beef.

A car pulled into a spot in front of him and the man behind the wheel parped his horn—to warn him to be careful or to say *hello*, Dash couldn't tell—and then he got down from his car and lifted his hat.

Dash was breathing rapidly. There were people walking here and there. A woman's heels clicked along the sidewalk behind him. A dog barked somewhere. It was just a regular Tuesday morning . . . in 1926.

There was a bakery across the road. The Rosshall Bakery. Its window was full of loaves of bread sitting naked on wooden shelves tilted toward the street. He looked both ways and crossed, almost in a trance. His belly went *gurrrrnk* and he covered it with his hand.

"Shh," he said to it, going inside.

There were customers—mainly women—standing in front of the glass display cases with little paper tickets in their hands. He took one from the red metal dispenser on the wall and stood with them. He watched as each person in turn selected their breads and pies and buns and cookies and cakes. Some had their bread sliced to order, some bought little cardboard containers of breadcrumbs. Each order was carefully wrapped in white paper and slid into a bag or arranged in a box and tied with white string, and each one made his gut squirm more. Finally, his number was called. He stepped up to the counter.

"Two hot cross buns," he said, having noted that they were two for three cents. He had nickels in his pocket: maybe nickels were still nickels.

The lady serving him used a pair of silver tongs to slide two buns out of the case and onto a tower of white paper sheets. She folded the paper around the buns and put them into a bag.

"Three cents," she said. He put his coin on the counter. She swept it up. "Your parents know where you are, sweetheart?"

"I'm visiting," he said. "That's why I'm not in school."

She looked at the money. "What is this?"

"Five cents."

"Is this American money, sweetheart?" She inspected the coin a little more closely, and he could see her face changing.

"Oh, my mistake—it's a souvenir from—"

"Where are you visiting *from*, young man? This nickel says it's Canadian . . ."

"Um, Montreal? You don't have the new nickels yet?"

"Montreal."

"Yes," he said, very quietly.

She looked like she'd made a decision. She passed the coin back to him, then leaned down into the case and picked up a flakey-looking pastry sprinkled with big sugar crystals. "Do they have these in Montreal?"

His stomach almost shot out of his nose and ran over the counter. "Oh, uh, not yet."

"No cherry purses in Montreal?"

"I don't think so."

"Why don't you have one as a souvenir of Toronto," she said, and she gave him the cherry purse along with the hot cross buns.

She looked at him a little funny, but not like he scared her or anything. He thought maybe she was reacting to his clothes or his haircut. He wanted to stuff everything into his mouth at once. Something below his ear was painfully throbbing.

"Thirty-two!" she called, looking away. "Thirty-two, please!"

Dash walked out to the sidewalk, cleared the bakery window, and then shoved the entire pastry into his mouth. Big soft cherries burst hot and juicy in his mouth. He chewed it like a bear, moving his jaw around to accommodate it all. A kind of blissful relief spread through him, like warmth filling a room. He felt his head clear. He swallowed and licked a couple of sugary crumbs off his fingertips.

"That's the best thing I've ever eaten!" he said aloud.

Some people looked at him. He didn't care. The hot cross buns lasted exactly a minute longer.

He continued east along the Danforth. A clock in a window said it was 11:55. He was supposed to go—if he *liked*—to that house in four hours. He'd already decided: no chance. But . . . he was curious. He knew most of the streets that let out onto Danforth Avenue, and Arundel was right in the middle of everything.

He walked up to number 64 and stood across from it. It was scrunched up between two other houses. All the curtains were drawn. There was no way he was going to knock on that door. He didn't linger, in case someone was watching him through a crack in the drapes. He went back down to Danforth Avenue.

People continued to scurry along the street. It was lunchtime now and ladies stepped nimbly over the streetcar tracks; men passed by holding their fedoras down on their heads. Some of the women had fur collars on their jackets. All the hats! Many of the men had large, furry beards. It was hard to see their faces.

And there was a gas station *right* on the sidewalk! British American Gasoline. He'd seen old gas-station commercials where boys with freckles and white-billed caps washed windshields with white cloth serviettes. A nickel thumb-flicked into the air afterwards. There was a kid of no more than fourteen using a pump that looked like a baby bottle with a glass top. It was all strangely close to the sweet old-timey images he'd seen now and again, but at the same time, there was something scary about it.

A voice was calling to him. Not just in his head, but an actual man's voice. He was saying, "Hey! Son?"

The man was wearing an apron over a suit and holding a pair of scissors. Dash took a big step back.

But the man was smiling. "Circus leave without you?"

"Beg your pardon?"

"Or are you just in from Prussia?"

Dash didn't know what to say. The man was looking up and down the sidewalk. "Where are your parents? They let you walk around in public with such majestic hair? And no hat?"

Dash took his eyes off the man long enough to look at the shop window. MILLS BARBER was painted on the glass. HAIRCUTS 25¢.

"You coming in, or are you going to risk capture by the Bald Men's Auxiliary? Come on now, I can't let you walk around in broad daylight like that."

He held the door to his shop open. Dash couldn't say no. In any case, no one had hair like his here—he'd have to get rid of it if he wanted to fit in.

He stepped into the barber shop. It was cool inside. There were two men waiting in chairs and a boy already sitting in front of one of the mirrors, where another barber was working on him. The boy had black hair, too much of it, and on one side it had already been trimmed back to his ears and thinned out. He shot Dash a glance through the mirror and then ignored him.

The barber pointed. "Take a seat, son."

One of the men waiting there said, "Looks like an emergency, Tom. He can go before me."

"Me too," said the other man. "I'm curious what he looks like under all that."

The barber—Tom Mills—gestured to his empty chair. "I'll take you next, then."

"I don't have any money," Dash said under his breath.

"When you find your parents, you can come back with your quarter. Can I trust you?"

"Yes, sir," Dash said quietly, reluctant to lie.

"Then up you go."

He draped Dash in a black, silken sheet, the sort of material magicians used. This kind of trick was called a *transformation*. Turn a boy from 2011 into one from 1926. The barber went to work, snipping back and forth, and big hanks of dark brown hair fell from his head.

The other kid was almost done. His barber was swishing at the back of his neck with a huge brush that looked like an animal's tail. "That's it, young Gibson," he said.

"Thank you, Mr. Jeffers," said the boy, who was about Dash's age. He put a quarter on the countertop.

"Walter . . . your father usually sends you with an extra nickel . . ."

Walter Gibson reluctantly dug the man's tip out of his pocket. The 1920s nickel was different than the one in Dash's pocket. Same size, but it was shaped like a stop sign.

The kid brushed at his pant legs. Then he stood and looked Dash square in the face. "Naw, I think he came from the rodeo, Mr. Mills," he said. "Left his cowboy hat on his horse, is why he ain't got a hat!" The boy laughed and the other men chuckled good-naturedly. "Looks like you cut him already," he added, pointing at a dot of red on Dash's cheek.

Dash glanced in the mirror and swiped at his face. "It's only cherry juice," he said, with a twitch of annoyance. "You never seen cherry juice?"

"I seen cherry juice! Whaddya think? I'm stupid?"

Dash turned his head to look at him directly, and a wave of fear swept through him. Mr. Mills had to stop cutting his hair.

"Do I know you?" Dash asked.

"Golly, I hope not," said the other boy. He gave Mr. Mills a sarcastic look and then pulled a cloth cap down over his new haircut and went back out into the street.

Dash turned to face the mirror again, listening to the sound of the scissors and watching himself be transformed.

"Trust me," said Mr. Mills, "you're better off steering clear of that Gibson boy. You being all new to town and everything."

A few minutes later, the barber whipped the satin apron off him, and there he was, his hair short and tidy and brushed back off his forehead. "Twenty-five cents, huh?" he asked.

"Just bring it when you can," said Mr. Mills.

He had a strange feeling when he got back out onto the sidewalk, and it wasn't just the cool air on the back of his neck. He felt more solid now. Like bits of him were still arriving. And that kid—Walter Gibson—he'd seen him somewhere. He was sure of it.

He was walking east now, lost in thought. What was he supposed to be doing here? Surely not eating pastries and visiting salons. Too bad neither of his parents had been born in Toronto or maybe he could get help from one of his grandparents. But were they even alive in 1926? Anyway, his mum's parents had lived in Winnipeg, and his father's were born in Thunder Bay.

He was lost in these thoughts when a fist came out and grabbed his shirtfront. He put his hands up in helpless defence as someone dragged him into the mouth of an alleyway.

"What's the big idea?" said Walter Gibson.

"What idea?"

"You, sassing me in front of Mills and Jeffers. You think I'm some kind of softie you can make fun of?"

"I didn't, uh, sass you."

"Say, you think you know me?"

He was pulling Dash closer, like he was going to bite him. His blue eyes flashed with anger. Dash could smell the oil Mr. Mills had put in his hair.

"Why would a guy like me know a kid like you?" He took his hat off and stuck it into his back pocket. He let go of Dash and put up his fists. "So now, you gonna apologize?"

"Holy crap!" said Dash.

The other boy's face blanched and all the fight went out of it. "Jeepers, you got a mouth!"

"I know where I know you from!"

"What're you—?"

Dash fumbled in his pocket for the envelope. He yanked the newspaper out and unfolded it. "Look," he said, offering it to the boy. "That's you, standing along the wall. With your brand new haircut."

That's where he'd seen him—in the photo of the Houdini lecture. Walter Gibson was one of the kids standing along the side wall. He was wearing the same hat in the picture that he'd just stuck in his back pocket!

"That's not me."

"That's your exact, brand new haircut. And that's your face. That's you, in Montreal."

"Ha!" said Walter. "I've never been to Montreal."

"Not yet. Look at the date." He pushed the piece of newsprint back toward the other boy.

Walter looked at the date and half closed his left eye. "Nice try," he said, handing it back. "Where are you from, anyway?"

"Nearby."

"Uh-huh. How old are you?"

"I'm eleven."

"And how many months?"

"I'm almost twelve."

"I'll be twelve in five months."

"I guess I'm older then."

Walter folded his arms over his chest.

"You never said your name."

"Oh. Dashiel. Woolf," he added. "Like a dog."

"A wolf is not a dog."

"But they're related."

"I know that," Walter said. "And I know you can't have a newspaper that hasn't been printed yet. So see ya." He walked out the mouth of the alley.

"Wait! *Look!*"

Walter turned with a snarl. Dash held the paper out.

"You're in the audience at a talk by *Harry Houdini*. Doesn't that interest you?"

"Not in the least!"

"Then explain why you're watching his lecture in this newspaper picture! Someone gave me this, and then I run into you . . . Don't you think that's something?"

"I think you're barmy."

"Well, I'm telling you—"

"See ya," said Walter, and he turned on his heel.

"No! Hold on!" Dash ran to catch up with him. "Look," he said nervously, "just listen for a second. I know it's going to sound a little crazy—"

"You think?"

"I'm from the future," he said. "I was in a magic trick that went wrong!" The other boy quickened his pace. "Just stop—listen to me! I think . . . I think that—"

"What!" Walter stopped suddenly and put a hand up at arm's length. "What do you *think*?"

"I think that, uh, you're supposed to go to Montreal. Like, tomorrow."

Gibson nodded, a little wild-eyed. "Sure, I am. For tea and crumpets."

"No."

"Then why?"

"I . . . I don't know why yet."

In a voice smouldering with anger, Walter said, "Get away from me!"

He moved off quickly, only looking over his shoulder when he'd put some distance between them. When he saw that Dash wasn't following, he slowed down. But Dash trailed him at a distance, ducking into shadow if the other boy turned around. They crossed through the big park (that was the forest Dash had seen at the end of Victor Avenue) and along Frizzell Avenue. Walter turned and went into a house.

Dash waited a minute, then he walked directly up to the door and knocked. It opened, and the boy stood there on the other side of it, looking dumbstruck. A man and a woman sat in the kitchen at the end of the hallway, staring at them.

"Have you got anything to eat?" Dash said to Walter, quietly. "Because apart from a cherry purse and a couple of hot cross buns, I haven't eaten in eighty-five years."

6

Walter Gibson bared his teeth. *"What are you doing here!"*

"I'm not crazy!"

The other boy looked out to the street, suspicious. "I said you were *barmy*, but it doesn't matter," he said. "I don't care what you're peddling. Find someone else to tell your stories to."

He was shutting the door when a deep, male voice said, "Walt, who's there?"

"No one, sir."

A man with a severe face appeared in the doorway. He leaned on a crutch that was tucked up under his arm. "Who are you?" he asked Dash.

"I'm a friend of Walter's."

"He's not, honestly! I don't know'm at all."

"Well, then, you have the wrong house," said Walter's father, and he began to close the door.

"Wait!" said Dash. "Hey, Walt, remember you were telling me you had an extra nickel and we were going to get some suckers?"

Walter's eyes widened so quickly they almost made a sound.

"Remember?" said Dash.

The man put one of his thin, pale hands on his son's shoulder and opened the door fully. He said, "What nickel is he talking about?"

"Nothing, sir," Walter muttered.

"Did you give Jeffers his tip?"

"Yes, sir."

"And do you know this boy or not?"

"A little. I know him a little."

The father gave his son an icy glare as he limped backwards into the foyer. Dash noticed that the bottom half of one of his pant legs was empty. It swayed a little as he moved.

"Your sister is asleep," Mr. Gibson said. "I expect the two of you will conduct your business quickly and in silence. Where is your hat?" he asked Dash.

"I lost it."

"And what kind of cufflinks are those?"

"Oh—these? Um, they're hockey sticks." He'd forgotten that he'd done his cuffs up with the little silver hockey sticks his grandmother had given him last year.

"Honestly. Children these days." Mr. Gibson turned and disappeared through a door.

Walter leaned in toward Dash and said, "Get goin'! Now."

His mother came into the hall. "Hello there, dear," she said. "What is your name?"

"Dash."

"Dash is going," said Walter. "He's gotta *dash*. Too bad. He would have loved to have more time for his visit."

"No time for pie?" Mrs. Gibson said, turning down her lower lip.

"I have to get back to school!" protested Walter.

Walter's mother put a hand lightly on Dash's shoulder. "School doesn't start for twenty more minutes. Now, who is your friend, dear?"

"He's new to the neighbourhood," Walter said through gritted teeth.

"Oh, welcome, then!" Mrs. Gibson said, bestowing a smile. It was so warm that Dash wanted to fold himself into her arms.

"Will you have a piece of quince pie?"

Quince? "Oh yes, thank you."

"Whipped cream?"

He could barely reply. "*Please*."

A few minutes later, Walter's mother ushered the boys out to the garden with two plates of pie. When he heard the door shut with a *snick*, Walter rounded on Dash and shoved his plate at him.

"What's the big idea, follering me to my *house*?"

"I have to talk to you."

Gibson shook his head. "Just eat your pie and scram."

"Look at the picture again."

"It's not me."

"Then look at this." He took a two-dollar coin out of his pocket, dated 2010. He gave it to Walter, who held it in his palm and stared at it.

"Big deal. Somebody gave you a medal."

"It's not a medal. It's a coin. Look at it! How could I fake something like that?" As Walter examined the coin, Dash tried to imagine seeing a toonie for the first time—the silver-coloured metal surrounding a smaller, yellow disk, like two coins in one. It was pretty impressive.

"That's easy," said Walter. "Get a coupla bits of scrap, some steel, some copper or brass, get someone to machine 'em for you, someone else cuts a hole in the big piece, you hammer in the smaller one. There ya go, there's your *coin*."

"C'mon," said Dash, "look at the date on it. And look, here's another one." He dug in his pocket for all the coins he'd had when he went onstage at the Canon Theatre. He'd bought the wine gums with a five-dollar bill his dad had given him, and he still had the change. There were a couple of dimes, a quarter, and some pennies. He recited the dates as he passed them over to Walter. "Dime, 1997; dime, 2006; two pennies, one from 1994, the other from 2009. Then there's another dime, an older one—look at this one, from 1981."

"I DON'T CARE!"

"Come on! Look at them! That's where I got that piece of newspaper, Walter. I got it in the *future*. In 2011."

Walter appeared uneasy. Dash knew how he felt. During the pause he took a big forkful of the pie and almost started singing. He didn't know what quince was, but it was softly sweet, a taste between lemon and cream. He got the newspaper page out again.

"I think this really is *you*," he said between bites.

Walter looked a long time at the image, and then his jaw dropped. "Oh no," he said quietly.

"What?"

He handed the newspaper back, looking away. "You're in it too. Your stupid cufflink."

Dash ran his eyes over the picture again until he saw the telltale glint of the hockey stick poking out from the sleeve of his suit jacket—the one he was wearing this very moment. His face was hidden behind Walter's shoulder, but that was him all right.

Walter took Dash's plate away. "I don't know how you did this or how you got here, but I want you to leave my house, and don't come back. And don't ever talk to me again."

"You boys done?" came a voice from the doorway.

Dash grabbed Walter's wrist before he could escape back into the house. "I live at 94 Victor Avenue. In an empty house. I have no money I can spend here and I have no idea how long I'm going to be stuck here!"

"Let go of me!"

"At least bring me some food! Okay? I know you believe me now!" The other boy pulled away. "Walt! Help me!"

Walter went to the door, where his mother was waiting.

"Come in, but keep it quiet," Mrs. Gibson said.

Dash thanked her, and she offered him that smile again.

"Oh, there you are, sweetie," she said.

He wasn't sure who she was talking to until he saw a girl of about six shuffling sleepily into the kitchen. She was grinding a fist into one of her eyes, and her mouth was turned down into a dramatic frown. Her expression said: *I'm sick!* She pulled out a chair from the kitchen table and sat in it heavily.

"This is our poor little Dee Dee," Mrs. Gibson said. The girl's hair was messy and her eyes were red. "She has a *terrible* cold." She kissed the girl on the forehead and frowned.

Just watching her made Dash feel sleepy.

"I am rather unwell," said Dee Dee. "My mother has given me a syrup that will make me feel better."

"I'm glad," said Dash. He could see Walter standing down the hall in the foyer, waiting to see him out. Or maybe *punch* him out. The kid was steaming mad. Dash leaned back into the kitchen. "Hey, Dee Dee? Would you like to watch a magic trick?"

"Yes, that would be very nice," said the girl. "Seeing as I am sick and in need of a distraction."

Dash looked back down the hall at Walter and tried to flash him a friendly little smile before he took a step *away* from the exit. He showed Dee Dee a quarter as Walter inched toward the kitchen.

"Now watch this coin," Dash said, placing it in his left palm. He put the date face down.

Dee Dee stared at the quarter, her eyes a little glassy. "I am watching it carefully," she said.

"Here it is, lying in the palm of my hand," he said. He waved his right hand over the coin. "Do you still see it?"

"I do."

He repeated the gesture over his upturned palm two more times. "Once . . . twice," he intoned, and the third time his hand passed over the coin, it had vanished. "Gone," he said.

Dee Dee made a small *O* with her mouth. "The most important thing about vanishing something," Dash said, "is making it come back." He leaned over, pulling the coin from behind her ear. "Tell your brother," he whispered to her, "if he wants to learn this trick, I can teach it to him."

The little girl was speechless.

Dash went up to Walter and put the quarter into his palm. Then he saw himself out.

There was nothing to do but go home and wait. And *worry*. Dash started across the park, like he would have done if he'd been coming from Alex's house on Wroxeter instead of Walter's on Frizzell. Though, he would never come home from Alex's house on Wroxeter again because Alex now lived in Leiden. Which was in Holland.

There were people in the park as the sun was high now. This was the warmest it had been since Dash arrived. The snow that had fallen the night before had mostly disappeared, although there were woolly tufts of it here and there on the grass. Two children were chasing each other around a large stone. One of them was crying, *Hey, lolly lolly!* They weren't so different, he supposed. Except for their get-ups, they were still kids.

"Surrender!" shouted someone from across the road. It was a little boy with a pop gun. He was shooting at Dash and feeble blue sparks flew up from the gun's muzzle.

"You got me," said Dash, feigning death with his hands over his heart.

"I am a' arm of the law, mister! Don't mix'er up with me!"

There was actual smoke coming from the gun. The kid blew it and walked off. Dash saw he had a cardboard star pinned to his shirt.

He crossed the park and continued toward his house. What was there to do in an empty house? He had to conserve energy. He couldn't keep walking around. Still, facing that house with its echoing rooms in the daylight—for some reason that freaked him out more than hearing himself laugh in it at night. He reversed his steps and began walking again up to Danforth Avenue. Maybe he'd find a pear tree or something. There were a lot of fruit trees in his neighbourhood. But the road he was on didn't seem to have any.

He moved at an easy pace through the quiet afternoon. The shops that had closed for lunch were just beginning to open again. *How civilized*, his mother would have commented. He looked at the theatre close to the end of Danforth that had been there forever. He couldn't remember what it was called in his time, but here it was a cinema, called the Century. It looked much more impressive than he remembered it. The marquee, sticking out over the sidewalk, announced what was playing: WHEN LOVE GROWS COLD and SO THIS IS PARIS.

But it wasn't a cinema every night of the week: a line at the bottom of both sides of the marquee said, TUESDAY NIGHT VAUDEVILLE PROGRAM: 25¢.

There was a card behind a glass window to the right of the ticket booth. It told who was starring in all the movies that week, and then, in a black box at the bottom, it listed the players in the vaudeville show.

TUESDAY NIGHTS AT THE CENTURY VAUDEVILLE FROLIC—10 ACTS!

JUGGLERS AND ACROBATS
Knickerbocker Singers, direct from Hoboken, N.J.

"THE FALL OF EVE"
a new one-act comedy

PATHE NEWS
MISS MERLE AND HER FEATHERED FRIENDS
The Act Deluxe of Birdland

BOONE HELM AND LIBERTY SLEPPO MASTER MARKSMEN

BLUMETHAL AND WOLFGANG
Performers of the Mysterious
Exclusive Photoplay
"CHARMING" MISS MARY MILES IN HER WINNING WAY

8PM, 25¢ Admission all seats

Suddenly his hands were tingling. Blumenthal?

BLUMENTHAL!

Tonight.

But where was he going to get a quarter? One he could actually use in 1926?

7

Late on a fall afternoon in the distant past, Dashiel Woolf sat in his empty bedroom and stared at the wall. If school worked here as it did in his own time, Walt would be getting out around now. Then he'd see if his new "friend" would bring him so much as a banana.

At around what must have been four o'clock, Dash at last heard the door downstairs creak open. He went to the top of the stairs and was about to call down when he heard the voice of a woman. She was saying,

". . . and enter into the gracious front hall, with rooms arranged in spokes around it . . ."

Dash flattened himself to the wall. He listened to at least three people moving beneath him.

"Dining room—certainly you could fit a table and have service for eight around it"—*ten*, thought Dash—"and here is a door that communicates directly with the kitchen behind, which"—she paused for effect—"is a *beautiful*, modern kitchen with a brand new four-compartment Bohn icebox . . ."

"Ooh," said a voice. "I like it, Mummy! Is *this* our house?"

"Now, dear, Daddy and I are looking at a lot of—"

Dash crept back into his bedroom and closed the door quietly. He was sure his thudding heart could be heard from downstairs. He had to get out of there, but he'd break his legs if he jumped from the second floor. Maybe there was grass. He stole a glance out the window. No, no. What was he, *barmy*? Maybe he could run out the front door while the family was busy in another part of the house. He opened the bedroom door again, but they were coming up the stairs! He saw their long shadows stroking upwards against the curving wall beside the steps. The girl was a lot younger than he, probably three, and her long black hair fell to either side of her neck in pigtails. He went back into the room and stood with his fist on the doorknob.

"Three bedrooms," said the agent. "One for the two of you, one for Adele, and one for whoever is coming next!" There was warm laughter.

He backed up toward the window and tried to lift the inner pane. Maybe he could climb onto the roof and wait. And what if he fell off the roof? Now they were in the hallway.

"Which is my room, Mummy?" came the girl's voice.

"Let's go look first at the master," said a male voice, friendly and stern all at once. They walked by the door.

Dash scooped up all of his belongings and threw them into the closet. They lay there as plain as anything but there was nowhere else to put them. And then he realized he had nowhere to put himself either, so he got into the closet too.

"This could easily be Adele's room," said the agent, entering. "With a desk under the window, and her bed right here in the corner."

"Oh, it's lovely, Trevor. Don't you like it?"

"Very roomy. What is the asking, again?"

"Sixty-two."

"Wow. That's a lot of money," the father said. There was a brief silence and Dash heard them move closer to the other side of the closet door. Trevor spoke quietly. "I thought we were going to try to keep it under fifty-five, Lois."

"Do you know what this house will be worth one day?" said Lois. "You won't think twice of spending sixty-two hundred dollars when we sell it for *twenty thousand*."

"When's that? Two thousand and six? When we're a hundred?"

He moved away. Dash heard the lady sigh. Then they all followed the agent back into the hallway, and she was saying, "Perhaps it will go for less, but I doubt it. I heard of a house on Logan that went for *seven thousand*."

And then he was alone again. He'd been breathing so shallowly he was beginning to feel light-headed. It was getting hot in the closet. He pushed the door open a hair. He felt the cool, fresh air rush in. He opened it another crack, half an inch. Then he saw the shoe. The little, black polished shoe. Just the side of it.

"Are you bad?"

The girl was standing in the middle of the room, holding the head of a doll in her hand. She was turning it thoughtfully. "No," he said. "Are you?"

"Mama and Papa are buying a house. This isn't your house."

"I'm just here for a couple of minutes," he said.

She fixed her huge brown eyes on his. She wasn't half as scared as he was. With a look of serious consideration on her face, she began twisting her upper half to the left and right. "Do you *live* in there?"

"Um, yeah. For now."

"Where do you make tinkle?"

"I think I hear your mum calling you."

She left the bedroom. He heard her voice out in the hall. "There's a boy in that room!" she called out gaily, and everyone ignored her. Then their voices faded as they all went back downstairs to the main floor, and out into the front garden.

Dash breathed slowly. The voices rose around the side of the house. He came out of the closet and warily looked out the window. The agent—a lady in a shiny black fur coat—led the family into the backyard. The mother was very pregnant and she held Adele's hand. The father, it seemed, was no longer interested in the property. He smoked a cigarette and walked behind them with a distracted manner. As they passed out of his view, the girl turned around and looked at him through the glass.

Then he heard footsteps clomping back up the staircase and he lunged for the closet again.

"Kid? Are you still in here?"

Walter.

"First bedroom at the top of—"

"Come on," Walter said, appearing in the doorway, "better

getcher stuff before they come back round the front!" He spotted the clothes on the closet floor and grabbed them.

Dash ran out to join Walter in the hallway and he stood at the top of the stairs.

"What made you change your—?"

"I brought you an apple, some bread, and two boiled eggs. That's all I could get out of—"

"Oh god, can I have it please?"

It must have been the look on Dash's face that caused Walt to stop right there and get the food out. Dash ate the apple in about three bites.

"Jeepers," said Walt. "Don't give yourself a tummy ache." The voices were coming around the front again. "Is there a back door to this place?"

Dash gestured with his head and the two boys continued down the stairs. "*To your left!*" He passed Walter to lead him through the kitchen and toward the mudroom. The possible future-owners of 94 Victor Avenue had come into the foyer, and Dash threw the back door open just as the agent came back through the front door. Walter and Dash snuck into the back-yard and hid behind a chestnut tree. They craned their necks around either side of the tree and watched the house.

After a minute, Walter retreated out of sight and beckoned Dash to join him. "That girl saw me," Dash said. "She thought I was a ghost."

"As good a guess as any." Walter was staring at him. It was hard to read his expression. He said, "Show me the trick."

"What trick?"

"The one you showed my sister."

Dash got a quarter out of his pocket. He let Walt see it before he put it into his palm. Then he waved his hand over it—"Once, twice . . ."

Walter grabbed Dash's hand, the one that was doing all the waving. The coin was still in his palm. Walter stared at it. Then, still holding Dash's wrist tightly, he looked up into his eyes. "I'm not your friend, you know."

"Fine," said Dash.

"I don't *have* to do anything for you."

"I know."

"Finish it."

Dash waved his hand over the coin for a third time, and it was gone.

"Again," said Walter.

It took him a while to get the whole technique, but by the time Dash was finished showing him (for a fifth time), Walter could do it fitfully. It wasn't smooth or convincing, but he seemed to have the basic mechanics.

"It takes practice," Dash reassured him.

Walt shrugged. The agent and her clients were gone now and the house was quiet. Dash led Walter back in and took him through to the foyer.

"This is the front hall," Dash said. "There's a table here." He held his hand about three feet off the floor, laying it on top of the phantom table. "This room is the dining room, but usually we eat in the kitchen. My mum bought a chandelier made out of antique chef's knives. It's nicer than it sounds. My dad calls it the Chandelier of Death by a Thousand Cuts."

"Do you really see a table and chairs?" Walter asked, squinting suspiciously with his left eye.

"No," he said. "There's nothing here. This is an empty room."

"This is an empty *house* . . ."

"I know. But I *will* live here one day. This is the only house I've ever lived in." He went down the hall. Walter was watching him very carefully now. "This is the kitchen," he said. "This is the cereal cupboard. My dad does a lot of the shopping because his hours are more flexible than my mom's."

"Flexible?"

"She's a doctor."

"Your mother's a doctor. My *uncle's* a doctor."

"Women can be doctors, Walter."

"I know that. I'm just saying it's a coincidence."

"Oh," said Dash.

"You know, a cold breakfast isn't good for your digestion. My granny says you have to wake your stomach up gently."

"I have cereal and cold milk every day of my life. We have a lot of different kinds at our house. Corn Flakes, Oat Squares, Multigrain Cheerios, Fibre Plus, Oat Clusters, and Count Chocula on the weekends."

"Count—"

"It's a chocolate-flavoured cereal."

"Of course it is."

"It *is*. There's a cereal called Froot Loops too, and it's like strawberry and cherry and orange."

"It's 'like' that."

"Well, it doesn't taste the same as actual fruit."

"And there really is a chocolate-flavoured cereal?"

"There is."

The two of them were standing in front of the bare cupboard. Walter seemed to be keenly studying its emptiness.

"Cereal's here, bottles and cans are here," Dash said. "Jars with, like, pickles and spaghetti sauce in them. And this is the cracker shelf."

"Cracker."

"Dry biscuits?"

"Oh, Hovis and the like."

"Yeah, I've heard of those. At Chanumas, my parents put them out with cheese."

Dash left the kitchen and headed toward the hall stairs. "Chanumas?" said Walter, catching up with him.

"My dad is Jewish and my mum is Christian. So we celebrate both. You know, Hanukkah and Christmas. We call it Chanumas."

Walter narrowed his gaze. "I think you should be careful who you tell these things to."

"There's a lot more than female doctors and mixed-up holidays in my time, Walter. In my time, men can *marry* each other."

Walter laughed heartily. *That* was a good one. "And that was your bedroom upstairs?"

Dash led him back to the second floor and into his room. "I have a dresser against this wall, and a blue wooden bookshelf beside the closet there. And on that wall, just across, is another bookshelf. It has all my graphic novels and my adventure books and a complete collection of Guinness World Records going back to 2005, which is when I first got interested in it. Do you know what the record for living on a tightrope is?"

"*Where's* your bed?" said Walter, quietly. He was still standing in the doorway.

"It's right there."

"That's where you sleep."

"I keep my best hockey cards in a box underneath it."

Now Walter walked into the room, cautiously, as if something could spring out. His gait was heavy. Whatever it was about this room, or things Dash had said about his life, Walter Gibson's face was changing.

"How did it happen?" Walt asked. "How'd you . . . end up here?"

Dash said, "I'd better start from the beginning."

Walter Gibson's brows had beetled downwards and his lower lip was tucked up under his nose. "If even a little bit of that is true," he said at last, "I don't know *what* to think." He was staring at some spot on the wall.

It had taken Dash a whole half hour to get through the story. The theatre Walter knew as the Pantages. The boy backstage and the envelope. How he'd been chosen against his will to go onstage, and how he'd ended up here.

By the point in the story when Dash was encased in the bubble, the two boys were sitting against the wall, side by side, across from the bright window. When the bubble popped, Walt stood up and went to look out.

"And there was no one there," Dash said. "No one. No one on the stage, and no one in the audience."

"Whaddya do?"

"I was scared to get off the stage. In case, like, it was part of the trick and I just had to stand still for it. Then some mean guy with a flashlight chased me out and I had to run away. I thought I was dreaming at first. But then I was dreaming about things I've never seen, not even in photos—restaurants in houses and newsboys. I saw a cart full of coal!"

"You've never seen coal?"

"I think that's what it was. You burn it in a stove, right?"

"Yeah . . ."

"I'd never seen it before."

"Well, you're not dreaming *me*, I can tell you."

"I know."

Walt studied him for a moment, his face in shadow in front of the window, his arms crossed over his chest. "What are we supposed to do in Montreal? You 'n' me?"

"I'm not sure yet. But wouldn't you like to meet Houdini?"

"I guess so. But I don't know how you think we're gonna get there."

"Well, I know one other person in Toronto, and I'm thinking maybe he can help us. But I need twenty-five cents."

"He a lawyer or something?"

"No. A magician. Bloom's grandfather, in fact."

"The one who invented the trick."

"That's right. And he's playing at the Century in a couple of hours. If I can get into the show, I can go talk to him. Can you get me a quarter?"

"Use one'a yours!"

"I almost got arrested in a bakery this morning, Walt. I need a quarter from 1926 or earlier."

Walt twisted up his face. "I knew you'd ask for money sooner or later."

"It's a *quarter*."

"Well, I don't have that kind of money."

"Can you get it? From home?"

"My father'll tan me if I steal from him!"

"What about your mom? Maybe tell her I'm borrowing it. I'll pay you back."

"With what?"

"I don't know. How hard can it be to get a quarter?" Walter looked at him like he was crazy. "Come on, will you help me?"

Walt furrowed his brow. "Show me the trick one more time."

8

A small crowd had already formed along the sidewalk in front of the Century when Dash arrived at six thirty. Walt had told him that *if* he could get the money, he'd meet him out front. There was still an hour and a half until the show started, but Dash had been too antsy to sit at "home" staring at the walls.

People drifted along the sidewalk. Pretty girls in long dresses, men in evening suits. There was even the odd tuxedo.

He wondered if maybe Blumenthal would come in through the front doors and he could talk to him here, in front of the theatre. Maybe he looked like his grandson and Dash would recognize him. That would be a lot easier, and if Walt didn't show with the money—

But here was the Gibson kid, coming straight at him. Early himself, and with a manic expression on his face. He was *way* excited. He wore a clean pair of pants, a jacket, and a tie. There was a cloth hat on his head and one in his hand.

"Here," he said, handing Dash the hat. "To fit in better."

"Did you get the money?"

"Did I ever!" He opened his fist to show a bunch of shiny coins in his palm. "I know my dad keeps some change in his humidor. There's almost seventy cents here."

"Is he going to miss it?"

"When he discovers it, he will. But that won't be tonight."

"I don't want you to get into trouble."

"Do you need my help or not?"

"I *need* it," said Dash. "Thank you. That's cool of you."

"Cool?"

"Nice."

Walt smiled. He probably didn't get called nice all that often.

"And anyway," Walt said, "your magician guy'll give me the money back, won't he? When he learns what kind of trouble you went through to see him?"

"Yeah! I'm sure he will!"

"I have enough for a bottle of mints too."

Walt walked up to the window to buy the tickets.

The lady looked at him from her glass box. "Sold out," she said.

Walter's jaw dropped. "Oh, *gosh*!"

"Watch your *mouth*, Walter Gibson," the lady said. "Yes, I know who you are."

Walter lowered his head.

"Ma'am, listen. Miss—" said Dash, coming up to the window.

"Who are you calling miss, young man?" She stuck her head forward on her neck. Her face looked like one of those warty squashes that come out in October. "Are you a *friend* of this one?

He broke my window with a *rock*, you know. Not a baseball, like a normal kid, a rock."

"Well, I'm sure it was an acc—" Dash started.

"No accident," she said, with a sour look on her face. "He's a scoundrel."

"I *said* I was sorry."

"You still owe me and Mr. Davis a whole dollar to fix that window. The two of you were planning on coming to the show tonight?"

"Yes, ma'am," Walter said awkwardly.

"That means *you* must have a quarter, boy. Give it here." She moved the window block aside and stuck her long, thin hand through the opening. Walter put a quarter into her palm.

"Sorry," he said to Dash.

"That's still seventy-five cents you owe me!" She got up and flipped a sign in the window that read SOLD OUT. People behind them groaned. "Bring a dollar twenty-five if you two want to get in next week!"

She stood up and exited the little box office through a door in the back. Walter's shoulders sank. "I forgot she worked here."

"You're pretty famous in these parts."

"A buck for a window! I paid *some* of it . . . jeepers."

"We can't give up."

"Whadder we gonna do?"

"Follow me."

*

There was an open alleyway on the east side of the Century and Dash nipped into it. It was dark, but at the mouth there was a sign that said The Finest in Cinema Projection and beside that were a couple of painted faces. Dash recognized one of them as Charlie Chaplin's.

Behind the cinema was a gravel service road. Two young men were unloading ferns in pots and a couple pieces of painted scenery from a horse-drawn cart. They shuttled back and forth between the truck and a door in the back of the theatre.

"Grab a fern!" Walter said. When the coast was clear, they both ducked into the back of the cart and grabbed a plant.

"I saw this in a movie once, I'm sure of it," Dash said.

They walked the two heavy pots into the back of the theatre and put them down. Dash grabbed Walt's sleeve and pulled him aside. "In here," he said. He went through a door into a stairwell.

"What're we gonna do?" Walt asked.

"Come up with a plan."

Light filtered under the door and a bulb burned on a landing above. They heard another door open on an upper level, and footsteps came down.

"Follow me," Walter said, and he led Dash behind and under the stairs. It was darker there, and it smelled of mould. "Shh."

They sat there in the dark and waited. After a while, Walter gave a single *glurk* of laughter, and then he did it again, and Dash elbowed him.

"You want us to get found?"

"No," Walter said, but even in the dark, Dash could hear him smiling.

The rest of the time until curtain passed slowly, and every few minutes a small snort, followed by an urgently whispered *sorry*, came from Walter Gibson. Dash pressed his lips together and tried to remind himself that he was probably in mortal danger.

Finally, they heard some applause and then the sound of a voice. They couldn't make out what it was saying.

"I don't know if the program outside is the real order of the evening," Dash whispered. "If it isn't, Blumenthal could be on first."

"So let's try to get in."

"What if we get caught?"

"We'll say we're unloading ferns."

Dash thought about it. "Let's wait until we hear applause. You know, between acts. Then maybe there'll be a lot of people moving around and we'll blend in."

"Good thinking," Walter said.

They heard singing through the wall. Horrible, shrieky lady-singing. Then a man replied to her, singing in a rumbly, vibrating voice. Someone was playing a tinkly piano. At the next explosion of applause, the two boys slid out from their hiding place and walked through the door. Backstage swarmed with activity. The ferns were being moved deeper into the interior of the building and pieces of set were coming out. A large woman in a dress plastered with feathers came hurrying back, peeling her eyelashes off. "Thenk you, thenk you *very* much," she said in a plummy British accent to everyone who passed her, including those who had said nothing to her at all.

"Excellent rendition," Walter said to her.

"My deepest grrratitude," she said, rolling her *r*s. "I am always moved by the musical sensibility one finds in the Colonies. Now come along, Roland," she called to a tall, thin man in a tuxedo. He was mopping the sweat from his brow.

Dash and Walt carried on. Soon they were standing close to the wings where some other performers were waiting to go on. "Here," Dash whispered. "We can stand back here by the ropes and wait until it's his turn."

They settled back against the side wall where some thick ropes hung. The next act was a little playlet that the audience found uproarious, about a man who comes home to find his wife being "wooed" by another man, whatever that meant. All three of them chased each other around the stage, except for when they suddenly stopped and sang about their problems. Then more chasing. They came off as hot and sweaty as Roland had.

After that, there was a shooting demonstration by a couple of tall fellows in spurs and leather pants. Boone Helm and Liberty Sleppo: *expert shootists*. Their thing was keeping a tin plate airborne by shooting pellets at it. Helm shouted, "I et my old pardna, Liberty, don' make me etcha too!" They danced around each other going *bang bang*.

Walter was becoming exasperated. "Are you *sure* your magician is playing tonight?"

"I'm pretty sure."

"At least this hasn't *cost* you anything," Walt said.

"I told you— Hey, look."

The emcee was coming back on. He gave a little cough into the microphone.

"And now, it is the Century's distinctive pleasure to be able to offer to you next a magic act of such prosaic peculiarity, such paucity of pomp, indeed of such prestidigitory imPROBability, that I think you will agree it is one of the most impressive spectacles of its kind."

A muscular man in a soiled undershirt jostled Dash and Walter out of the way. "You two shouldn't be 'ere," he said, reaching to loosen a rope. A length of it zipped upwards, making a high zinging sound. Then, without another word, he moved on to his next task.

"To be sure," continued the emcee, "you have never seen such stylings as those of our next performer, the one, the only— please hold your applause!—*Blumenthal and Wolfgang!*"

He swept his arm off to his right—toward the other side of the stage—and a thin man emerged from the wings. He was a ragged-looking person of about thirty, with black hair down to his shoulders. He held a hand up to greet the crowd and a ripple of laughter went through it. He was rather handsome, but slight, and his sole apparatuses were a beat-up pasteboard suitcase and a folding table. He was the only person onstage. Dash didn't know if he was Blumenthal or Wolfgang.

The man came to centre stage and flicked the table open.

One of its four legs had been repaired with rope and a tree branch. The table wobbled, and he had to put the suitcase to one side to steady it. It was something of a balancing act, but after a moment or so he had it settled and he stood back, his hands open to catch it if it suddenly collapsed. Finally, he assumed the pose—somewhat—of a professional magician: his head held high, his hands out to his sides. The audience laughed again.

"Good evening," he muttered. He brought one of his arms sharply forward and made a fist. Nothing happened. He gestured with the other hand, and a tiny spark of red appeared atop his fist. It spread. It was a petal. Another appeared.

Of course, Dash thought, *the magic rose.*

Blumenthal circled his fingers over his fist and the whole bud showed on top of it. Then the stem appeared, and he winced comically as the thorns poked out one by one. At last he held a single, long-stemmed red rose in his hand. He passed it to a woman in the front row, but to just a smattering of applause. Disappointment flickered across the magician's face.

Now he gestured broadly at his suitcase and made a sort of bow. He raised the suitcase's lid, propped it up, and removed a cheap-looking magic wand. He began to wave it but became distracted by something in the case and reached forward and stirred the air. The wand flew out of his hand and vanished into the suitcase. The lid slammed shut and the makeshift table collapsed.

Walt looked at Dash. *This is the guy who's supposed to send you home?*

The magician muttered and set up his equipment again. When he opened the suitcase a second time, the wand suddenly poked out of it and he took hold of its end. But something in the suitcase had the other side. The man struggled with the wand, wiggling it back and forth, and then a grey squirrel's head popped out of the case. It had the other end of the wand in its mouth. They heard it chittering angrily, yanking hard on one end of the wand as the magician held the other. They were having a tug of war.

"No, Wolfgang!" the man shouted. "Hey! *Hergekommen!*" The audience was shrieking with cruel delight. He rapped his knuckles on the open half of the lid to scare the squirrel into dropping the wand.

Dash put his head in his hands. It wasn't supposed to be funny, he could see that. Blumenthal was hopeless.

Wolfgang had bested his master. Now he was running all over the stage with the wand in his mouth, sassing him triumphantly. Blumenthal gave chase, but the squirrel was quickly up the curtain on the other side of the stage. Once at the level of the balcony, he leaped off the curtain and ran, tail twirling, along the railing.

"Uh, my fine ladies and gentlemen, I request your attention. Here, let me propose . . . I— Look here, in this hat of mine. I have a length of rope here— No reason to give that badly trained creature all your attention. Look how much rope is here in this hat."

Five pieces of dirty rope hung from one of his fists. No one was paying attention to him. Someone had turned a spot on Wolfgang as he sprung from balustrade to chandelier, from chandelier to wall sconce, the whole time holding the wand in his mouth and chirruping.

Blumenthal bravely soldiered on. Dash focused on him from the wings, moving a little closer to the stage. The man was showing the five ropes of differing lengths, yanking them taut between his fists, ignoring the gales of hilarity coming from the auditorium. His hands were steady. He took the five lengths and made two of them into one, and then he made two others into one, and then he balled the whole mess up into his hands and suddenly shook out a single rope, more than ten feet long. It lay on the stage, but there was only scattered applause.

He had done it well—usually, magicians did the rope trick with only three ropes, and it was hard enough that way—and Dash clapped for him and nudged Walt with his elbow.

Blumenthal acknowledged them with a surprised sideways glance into the wings, and then he paused, turned, and held his hand out toward them. But the audience had had their share of Blumenthal's act and his quarrelsome squirrel. They began to boo him.

"Now, now," he said. "Why don't we do some magic with rings for you nice people?" He reached his fingers into a vest pocket and took out a small, black steel ring. But the booing only increased. Blumenthal smiled out at them, and then replaced the ring in his pocket and clapped his hands twice. Wolfgang suddenly bounded back onto the stage and went right into the suitcase. The lid closed as the table rocked beneath it and

Blumenthal's wand rolled across the stage right to his feet. He picked it up, took the handle of the suitcase, and kicked the table closed with the toe of his battered shoe.

Then he took a low, gracious bow, and left the stage.

There were catcalls mixed in with a little applause.

"Did you see that?" said Dash.

"I did," replied Walter. "He was horrible!"

"We gotta talk to him!"

"He doesn't know what he's doing!"

"He does. He's a magician, he . . . he did the rope trick really well, don't you think?"

"You think *this* guy invented a time machine out of soap? He's rubbish. I'm going home." Walt started for the rear doors. "You better get me my quarter back."

Dash grabbed him by the elbow. "Come and see him with me."

"Why?"

"Because you're in this now." He looked straight into Walt's eyes. *"Aren't you?"*

"I don't know," said Walt. "Someone here is a bit goofy, and I think it's you."

"Maybe," Dash said. "But how will you know for sure if you don't stick around?"

Walt was looking highly unconvinced. "I'll go with you. Just to see what happens. If you're taking me for a ride, though . . . you're gonna regret it. I know fisticuffs!"

9

A pair of small dogs had taken the stage with their trainer, and they were jumping over chairs and standing on their hind legs. The boys went into the clamorous hallways behind. There was a warren of rooms scattered along its length, and Walter hesitated, flattening himself against a wall before a corner.

"Do you really know where to look for him?"

"He's gotta be back here somewhere." Dash retreated a couple of steps to stand beside him against the wall. "There's nothing to be afraid of, you know."

"I'm not afraid! Do I look afraid?"

"So come on, then—"

"I'm also no sucker," he said.

"There's no way I can outrun you, and I couldn't take a single punch from you, so why would I mess around? Look, he probably won't be here for long! And I can go on my own, but . . ." He shrugged. "It's, like, your loss, dude."

"What's like my loss? Dude?"

"Never mind." Dash snuck around the corner into the dark hall alone, but he knew—he had an instinct—that Walter Gibson would be right behind him. He took a few more steps before looking over his shoulder.

"Don't want anyone to take advantage of ya," Walt said. "You're not from around here."

They walked side by side, each checking the shadows for surprises, and soon they emerged from the other end of the hall into another dimly lit corridor. There were people here; a couple of the doors were lit from behind. A woman in a ballerina costume stood in front of them, smoking a cigarette, and behind her, two acrobats were stretching their muscles.

Dash whispered, "Look like you know what you're doing," and he stepped into the light. The dancer started. "Oh, excuse me, ma'am," he said to her. "We're just going to our dressing room."

"You boys frightened me," she said, with one hand against her chest. "What time are you on?"

"Soon," said Dash, walking past her.

"What's your act?" rasped a wiry-looking acrobat.

"Time travel," Walt said.

Dash began trying doors. In the distance, they heard the laughter of the crowd and then there was a drumroll.

"If I was him, I'd have made tracks by now, before the tomatoes ripen."

"You better hope he's still here," Dash said, "or you might be bringing me boiled eggs for the rest of your life . . ." He was about to knock on a door, when they heard a familiar-sounding voice from across the hall.

"Forget it! No, you are not getting an acorn right now, no. You've made a fool of me for the last time!"

Dash went to that door and knocked.

"What is it *now*?" came the voice, deeply aggrieved.

"Is that Mr. Blumenthal?"

"No one here but us *sqvirrels*."

"Please, sir," Dash said through the door, "may I speak to you, please? It's very important."

"Go away."

Walt pushed Dash aside. He put his mouth to the door. "Your rope trick was really . . . very splendid," he said. "Sir."

"Oh, well, humble thanks, then. Now go away." There was silence for a long moment, and then the door finally opened. The magician stood there in an undershirt, his suspenders hanging down on either side. "You didn't go away."

"You're a good magician. We were watching," said Dash.

"How old are you boys?"

They answered in unison: "Twelve—"

"—almost," Walt added.

"Well, thanks for the compliment, almost-twelve-year-old persons. Now, *so long*."

He began to close the door, but Walter put his palm against it. "Uh, could I just get an autograph, or something? Please, sir?"

Blumenthal stared at them through the half-closed door. "You liked the rope trick? The *furshlugginer* rope trick?"

"*Yes,*" said Dash. "It was a very *original* effect. Five ropes. I've never seen it done with five ropes."

"Yeah, how'd you do it anyway?" Walt asked.

Blumenthal stared at him through the crack in the door.

"You don't ask that," Dash said. "Mr. Blumenthal, did you invent that, um, version of the trick?"

"I did . . ." The door drifted open a little. He stepped back and it floated open all the way. He turned and went back to the dressing-room table, muttering to himself. "Is it too much to ask maybe a girl comes backstage and asks for an autograph? No, I get two boys who don't have *whiskers* yet, fulla questions . . ." They considered themselves invited and entered. "In Minsk I vanished *elephants*," he said, his voice strangling in theatrical anguish. "But here? They don't care. They want to look at a fat lady sing and two geniuses shoot a plate. Oh, but what is this? A rope trick with *five* ropes? No thank you."

"Did you train Wolfgang to do all that?"

"What train?" he said, shooting a nasty glare at the cage that sat on the floor. Wolfgang was curled up in the bottom of it. "He wants his own show! Such a big squirrel-about-town." He stared at the animal. There was a reluctant affection in his eyes. "For this I rescued you from Han Ping?"

"Han Ping?"

"He was riding *tricycles* for Han Ping! With a little top hat. Such dignity."

"Mr. Blumenthal?"

He looked back and forth between them. "What is it? Whaddya want?"

"I'm just wondering . . . why you don't do some of your . . . *other* tricks?" Dash asked.

"For these yankels? They wouldn't know a good magic trick if it jumped up and vanished on their nose."

"But you have other tricks, right?"

"Yeah, sure I do," the magician said, using a matchstick to pick his teeth. "I can make a ribeye disappear too."

"What about . . . ?"

"What?"

"What about your Soap Bubble Vanish?"

Blumenthal regarded the two of them with mild distaste. "My what?"

"Oh, bully," said Walter. "Hey, you don't have a quarter, do you?"

"The Soap Bubble Vanish," continued Dash. "I heard it was a special trick you did. That you invented."

Walter flung his hand out. "Aw, cantcha see? This guy couldn't get a rabbit out of a barn. He's an amateur!"

Blumenthal nodded sagely in the direction of Walter Gibson. "You want to know how to do a magic trick?"

"He already *taught* me one," Walt said dismissively. "He can make a whole quarter vanish right in front of your eyes!" He snapped his fingers. "Just like that."

"*I* want to know," said Dash. "That ring trick you were going to do—"

"Before you were so *rudely* booed off the stage," said Walt.

"Ah, the ring," said Blumenthal. "Let me see if I can find it." He went back to his chair and rifled in his vest, then brought the ring over for inspection.

Dash held it in his hand. Just a plain metal ring, tarnished from being handled, almost black. It was the circumference of a can of soup.

"Now," said Blumenthal, "how is a good magic trick done?" He took the ring back and held it out in the air between his thumb and forefinger. He moved a couple of steps away from them and gestured that they should remain still. "It is just a mixture of light, misdirection, tomfoolery, and mechanics." He held the ring very still in the air, like he was balancing it on something. Then he let go of it and it stayed there, floating. "Oh, and technique," said Blumenthal.

"Howdja do *that*?" asked Walt.

"With mirrors," the magician answered. "Here, look." He picked the ring out of the air and gestured them over to his mirror. There, he performed it again, and the ring hung in the air as well as in the reflection, just a foot away. He lit a candle. "Here now, get those lights," he said to Dash.

Dash turned out the lights and came back. Blumenthal held the candle behind the ring and it hung doubled in ghostly reflection.

"This is how it's done," said Blumenthal. "The one in the mirror is the real one," he said, and he shot his hand out toward the glass and snatched the reflected ring out of the mirror.

Walter went white and ran out of the room.

"You *are* the guy who invented the Soap Bubble Vanish."

"Sure, I am. And I invented horse-racing too." He *pshaw*ed and went to flick the lights on again. "Your friend has a weak constitution?"

"Please, Mr. Blumenthal. I came a long way to find you. The Soap Bubble Vanish *is* your trick. Maybe you . . . you just haven't invented it yet."

"How would you know that? You a medium?"

"A medium?"

"A person that talks to ghosts."

"No. But, um, I do know some things."

"Like what?"

Dash sighed. "Look. I was *in* a trick called the Soap Bubble Vanish, and it was a trick everyone said you invented. Something went wrong with it."

"It turned you into a terrible liar?"

"No. It sent me back in time. Eighty-five years, to be exact."

The minimal warmth in Blumenthal's eyes had faded. "Excellent. A comedian." He threw a soiled towel into his suitcase.

"Sir—"

"Ah-ah-ahh!" said Blumenthal, his index finger raised in warning. "We are finished, thank you very much. Goodbye." He stood and grabbed Wolfgang's cage in his other hand. "Say hullo to Gluckman for me."

"Gluckman?"

"Too late to play dumb. Herman Blumenthal wasn't born yesterday, all right? So long, kid."

Dash protested, "Wait—"

"*SAYONARA!*"

Blumenthal grabbed the case with all his effects in it and left the room. Dash stood there a moment, despondent, then trudged back out into the hallway. Walt was waiting at the end of it, by the rear exit.

"Thanks a lot," Dash said to him.

"That guy's a warlock."

Dash put his head in his hands. "I need to get home, and 'that guy' is the person who's supposed to do it! But I'm in Montreal *tomorrow*? Why?"

"I don't know!"

"Put on your thinking cap, Walt!"

Walt said, "Mine is already on, okay? Gosh, you're bossy!" And he exited through the door to the back alley.

That night, Dashiel Woolf felt he was truly alone in the universe. Nobody knew what was happening to him. The dark outside the curtainless window had distressed him the night before; now it overpowered him. He was lost in time and space.

He laid one of his dimes in the light and watched it gleaming, as if it were something alive to keep him company, and then he picked it up and began scraping his name in the brand new lacquer. He finished the *D* and stopped, unable to listen to the disturbing sound of the dime scraping against the floor of an empty house.

Finally, he fell asleep under his jacket on the wooden floor, his face in the little patch of moonlight coming through the window. His dreams were full of urgent voices. Bodies rushed one way and the other. He saw faces he knew and the faces of strangers. The world of his dreams was so chaotic that when he finally awoke, he was still exhausted. A gloomy orange light filled his room. At least the night was over.

He stood in the window and looked out toward the woods, and the sun was coming over them, setting the tops of the trees aglow. The red and yellow leaves were fierce in the light.

He was hungry again. Fear and hunger were things he'd only ever imagined until now. He knew that people in other parts of the world suffered from them. Every year in their house, they'd make a decision—the three of them together—what two charities they would send money to. His parents would write a cheque and Dash would forgo his allowance for two weeks and contribute. It was a good feeling to know the money he'd spend on hockey cards and comic books would, for those two weeks, be helping someone somewhere else in the world.

But now he needed help himself.

He put his jacket on and went downstairs. He stepped out into the crisp dawn air and took it deep into his lungs. Fresh air made you feel so alive, no matter how screwy the universe got on you.

Some of the men on the street were already getting into their cars to go to work, or walking out to Broadview with their leather briefcases hanging from their hands. There was a boy standing in a doorway across the street, waving goodbye to his father. Just a normal morning for them—

"*Yasas*, Papa!" the boy called. He was maybe six years old.

"*Yasoo*, Louie!" said the man as he got into his car.

Louie!

Same house too!

At ninety or so, Louie would wear his pants up to his rib cage, but today he was a little boy in his pyjamas waving goodbye to his papa.

Dash wanted to wait for the car to pull out and then go up to the little boy and say to him, *I'm Dashiel! I'm Dashy!*

Walt came at eleven, on his way home for lunch. He had another apple and one boiled egg with him, which Dash ate ravenously. He almost bit into the egg with its shell still on.

Walt watched him uneasily. "I was thinking last night."

"Yeah?"

"That Blumenthal guy. He doesn't know how to do this trick you need him to do."

"I know that."

"So maybe that's why you and me have to go to Montreal. To get Houdini's help."

Dash pushed himself off the bedroom floor and started walking around making silent gestures with his hands. "O. M. G.," he said.

"*Homegee?*"

"Never mind—I mean, you're right. We really gotta go."

"Yeah, but how?"

Dash stopped against the far wall, facing the closet. "Are there planes yet?"

"Yeah, there are planes, Dash. If you're a rich man. You got a hundred dollars or something in the bank?"

"We have to be there *tonight*."

"We'll take a train," said Walt.

"Oh, you have trains too!"

Walt just stared at him. "There have always been trains, skipper."

"Okay. Good." His mind clanked into motion. He felt the weight of a tennis ball in the upturned palm of his hand. He tossed it: nothing but net. Walt was getting used to his strange behaviour and hardly batted an eyelash.

"I think I know what we have to do," Dash said. "Do you ever have sleepovers?"

"Do you mean, have they been invented yet?"

"Can you leave your parents a note that you're, like, studying for a test and you're staying at a friend's house overnight? Like, give the name of a real person or something, someone who'll cover for you."

"I think, like, that might, like, work, Dash. Like."

"Okay."

"I can't get enough money for two train tickets."

"I think *I* can," replied Dash.

10

They checked the newspaper at a stand up on Danforth Avenue. There was a train to Montreal, today, at 1 p.m. There wasn't much time.

Dash insisted that Walter accompany him to the house on Arundel. There was no way he was going to knock on the door by himself and get chopped up into someone's stew.

On Arundel, Dash stopped about twelve houses up. "Hey, I just realized something."

"You're insane?"

"No. There are houses here."

"Of course there are."

"But in my time, *right here* is a parking lot. You won't believe this, but in the future there are going to be so many cars that leaving them somewhere when you're not driving them is going to be tricky."

"And they rip up houses so they can park them?"

"They rip 'em up to build roads too. And bigger buildings."

"They better not tear *my* house down."

"I don't think they have, Walt. At least not yet."

They walked up the other side of the street and stood across from number 64. The curtains were still drawn behind the streaky windows.

"You missed the party they wanted to throw you yesterday, and now you want to ask them for money?"

"Well, they seem to know me," Dash said. His stomach was aching with both hunger and worry. Maybe if the people in this house didn't come to the door wearing goalie masks and holding chainsaws, he could ask if there were any of those snacks left over.

They both took a deep breath and crossed the road. The front yard was overgrown with huge, dead weeds. Spikes and puffballs. "You knock," said Walt.

"Just stand right there," Dash said, indicating a spot on the porch one inch away from him.

He knocked.

Nothing.

He looked at Walt for moral support, but Walt only shrugged. Dash counted to five and then knocked a little harder.

He stepped back. He could hear someone inside coming down the stairs, then crossing the hall toward the door. The boards beneath him announced the approach of some substantial person. He felt frightened again. The window in the door shook and stirred the light.

Then it went dark. There was a face there, filling the glass pane: a big, white, round face with a long, bushy moustache and two very small black eyes. The eyes blinked at him. Dash stood frozen for a second. Then he fumbled in his suit-jacket pocket for the envelope.

"Hold on, hold on," he said. He took out the card with the typed message on it and held it up to the window.

The man unlocked the door and opened it. He'd been bending over to look out the window; now he straightened to his full height. He was a giant in a long grey sleeping shirt. It went almost all the way to his feet. Dash's mother had something like it in pink.

"I'm sorry," he said. "I didn't mean—"

"*Koyziti?*"

"Sorry?"

"No," said the man, and began to shut the door.

"Wait!" said Dash, holding his palm out to keep the door open a crack. "Does anyone else live here? Please?"

The man studied Dash's black suit. His eyes narrowed. "*Zosto shtey oblecheni kako schto?*" At least that's what it sounded like.

"Please . . ." Dash said. "*S'il vous plaît?*"

"*Francuski?*"

"No, English." There was an open door on a landing one flight up. Light was falling into the hallway there. "Does anyone up there speak English?"

A young boy of about eight came and stood on the landing. "Papa?"

"*Pomonkney ova momchee,*" said the man, and the boy came down the stairs slowly, taking Dash in with a worried look.

"Hello?" he said.

"Hello," said Dash. "Someone told me to come here."

"Who tells you?"

"They gave me a card with this address on it." He showed the card again. The father watched the two boys talking and eyed Walt out on the porch. Walt saluted. The man asked his son something.

"Are you American?" asked the boy.

"No. I'm from here . . . from Toronto. Who lives in this house?"

"My father and me live in one of the rooms. There is two families same floor and another family in basement. A man live by himself back there—" He pointed down the hall that stretched beyond the stairs on the main floor. "This room, no one live." Now he indicated the door to his left. "You want room?"

"No. I thought someone here was expecting me. Do you know all the people in the house?"

The boy spoke to his father. "My father say families are both Macedonia, like us, and the man who live alone is from Irishland."

"Can I talk to him?"

"No," said the boy. "He does work. Come home late at night."

"Where does he work?"

"Bricks," said the boy. "He make bricks."

Dash looked down at the card in his hand. There was no name, no instructions. No explanation at all. "I don't know what to do."

"Go home."

Dash stepped back out onto the porch. The father watched them carefully as he closed the door on them.

"I guess you missed the party," said Walt.

"Something is wrong. Who gave me this?"

"Well, if you'd gone when you were invited, maybe you'd know by now. Meantime it's almost noon. If we're not going to Montreal, I have to go back to school."

"No . . . wait," said Dash. "I have another idea."

It was one of those plans hatched in desperation and destined to fail. Dash was going to convince Herman Blumenthal that the Soap Bubble Vanish was *real*, and that he and Walt knew how to get it invented. But it was going to take a real master to bring it into existence. Houdini.

Once he explained that, how could Herman Blumenthal pass up the opportunity? To work with Harry Houdini? Blumenthal would buy them a couple of train tickets for sure. Maybe he'd even come with them! Once he saw the *Gazette*, he'd know Dash was telling the truth.

But first, they had to *find* Blumenthal, and that entailed locating a hotel with a phone "register" (as Walter had called it) that would show the magician's address. Addresses were in the register even if the people listed didn't have phones. The concept of phonelessness bewildered Dash. How did people ever get in touch with each other? If someone you knew didn't have a phone, did you have to *walk over to their house* to make plans? Did you have to *write them a letter*?

Walt had told him that at the top of the woods and across the park there was a series of streets with small houses. It was a neighbourhood of working people's houses, little red-and-yellow-brick dwellings with vegetable patches on the lawns. "Not a lot of money up there. You might stick out even worse than you did in my part of town. But there's a hotel on a street called Carlton up there. It's called the Queen's Arms. They might have a register."

They decided on Dash's outfit. He was going to wear one of Walt's shirts. His pants were fine. All of Walt's shirts took cufflinks, so Dash just used his hockey-stick cufflinks. He wore his suit jacket with the cloth cap Walt had given him the night before. While Dash was trying to find Blumenthal, Walter was going to go home and collect a few more items of food and clothing and leave a note for his parents, before making his way down to Union Station. He was going to be in a world of trouble, but he'd made up his mind.

They parted ways and Dash hoofed it up the steep hill leading to town. Then he headed into the warren of streets that led toward the main streets, one of which was supposed to be Carlton.

The side streets finally gave onto a broad, paved expanse of road down which streetcars progressed in a swaying, uncertain fashion. Then, just down a jot, he saw Carlton and made his way there.

The Queen's Arms Hotel was on the south side. A heavy glass lantern hung over the porch. He went through the door into the foyer, a cramped space with a wooden desk sticking halfway into it. A man was reading a newspaper in a comfy chair, and the man behind the counter let Dash use his register. After a few moments of riffling the pages, Dash found *H. Blumenthal*.

"Where's Augusta Avenue?"

"That's in the market," said the man over in the chair. Dash turned to see he'd removed the pipe he'd had clamped between his teeth. "You just take the Carlton tram over past Spadina. It's the first left after that."

"Left past Spadina?"

"That's it. Be careful. Not a nice part of town."

"Pickpockets and werewolves," said the counterman.

"I'll be careful," said Dash, pushing the directory back across the desk. Spadina. How long a walk was that? He hurried out the door. It couldn't be that far.

Twenty minutes later, he was goggling at the sight of a dozen houses standing where Maple Leaf Gardens was supposed to be. He didn't have time to think it over; he carried on. He was panting for breath and he wasn't halfway there.

It was already ten to noon. They had to make a train at 1 p.m. to get to Montreal in time for Houdini's talk. It was getting cold again. He crossed Yonge Street, looking south for a moment. He could see the Pantages sign hanging over the street, a little white droplet stuck to the side of a building.

There were lots of people here, as there had been Tuesday night, but most of them now were coming back from lunch, not going home. He dodged them, one way and the other, and pushed on. Bay Street, Queen's Park. A flag flapped in the light breeze, as it always did there, except it wasn't the Canadian flag. It was a red flag with the *British* flag in the corner.

Weird.

He arrived in Kensington Market. It was even dirtier and smellier than he remembered, and there were chickens clucking in wire cages stacked on the sidewalk and stray dogs sniffing in the gutters. He smelled coffee roasting and meat being broiled, and to one side of him was an open stall selling spices out of paper bags, to the other, a store with sausages hanging in links in the window. His stomach called out to them. The signs in all the windows were Hebrew.

Seventy-eight Augusta was a small bookshop and beside it a set of stairs led to a basement. Apartment B. He went down and knocked on the door.

Nothing.

He knocked again. No answer. Did anyone ever answer their doors in this town?

"MR. BLUMENTHAL! ARE YOU HOME?"

"Ohfer!" came Blumenthal's voice. The door flew open. His red eyes tracked down. "What the—? *You?* What are you doing here?" He slivered his eyes. "How'd you find me anyway? You *following* me? Gluckman tell you to follow me?"

"No!" said Dash. "I don't know any Gluckman! I just want to talk to you. It's really very important. I found you in the phone book, er, register."

Blumenthal narrowed his eyes. He was wearing a pair of soiled brown pants and an undershirt. "What is your name?"

"Dashiel."

He looked at the boy in his doorway and seemed to weigh his options. Then he stood aside and let Dash in. The apartment was a single room, small, and it smelled of cigar smoke. There was a couch with a discoloured white cloth over its back, and a table with three chairs. A pot of water was simmering on the nearby stove.

"Sit down," he said to Dash. "Give me that Phillie." Blumenthal was pointing at a standing ashtray to his right. There was a cigar in it. Dash passed it to him and Blumenthal held a match to it. Instantly the room filled with a fresh cloud of noxious, light-blue smoke. "Ahh, good," he said.

He went to his fridge and opened the door. Dash saw a little block of ice in the bottom, and a fur of frost around the opening. Blumenthal took out a wet package wrapped in waxed paper. He reached into a paper bag on his counter and took out a bagel, which he pried apart with his dirty thumbs and laid flat on his countertop. There was a small plate with some kind of bun coated in big square crystals of sugar. The sight of it made Dash's mouth water. Blumenthal plastered a thin layer of what came out of the wax package on each half of the bagel and handed one to him. He tried not to eat it too quickly, although from the way Blumenthal ate, Dash didn't think he'd mind if he shoved the whole thing into his mouth at once. The stuff in the package was cream cheese, but it was both dense and fluffy, and tasted more like cream cheese than cream cheese had ever tasted before.

"So, whaddisit already?" said Blumenthal. He tore a massive hunk out of the bagel with his front teeth and spoke through it. "For *what* do I owe this pleasure?"

"Can I show you something?"

"Gonna vanish a quarta' for me?"

"No," said Dash. "This—"

He held out the newspaper clipping. The man glanced at him with suspicion before taking it and unfolding it.

"What is this?"

"It's a newspaper that won't be printed until . . . tomorrow morning."

"Thanks," he said, handing it back. "But I don't read so good."

"Look," said Dash, pointing at the picture. "That's Walt. Who you met last night. And that's *me*. Standing beside him. Someone gave me this newspaper eighty-five years from now, and it has a picture in it of *me* and a kid I just met yesterday."

"Why do I care?" He looked up at the ceiling. "This is a question I find myself asking on a daily basis . . ."

"You should care because the reason we're in this picture is that him and me are in Montreal asking Houdini for his help."

"What help?"

"With the trick. The trick you're supposed to invent."

Blumenthal took a long drag on his Phillie, sucking the smoke in through the mess of bagel and cheese in his mouth. Involuntarily, Dash grimaced.

"You don't have to be stuck at the end of a Tuesday night vaudeville show!" he said urgently. "You're good! You should be doing your own act on a real stage!"

"HEY!" Blumenthal said, and now he sounded angry. "I don't need you and I don't need anyone to tell me howta do what I do! You think I take advice from a kid?"

"No."

"So *shaddap*."

Dash looked away from the man's red, angry face. "Who's Gluckman?"

"Gluckman," Blumenthal spat. "My thieving, lying *former* friend."

"Why former?"

"You ask a lotta questions."

"Just tell me. Maybe all this stuff is happening for a reason."

"*What* reason? You're just a kid. You don't know that things happen for *no* reason, not yet. You wanna know about Gluckman? He was my best friend. I knew him from the old country. Went to school with him. We killed chickens together fa goodness sake. So, who else are you going to trust with your life? He owns the Pantages, best stage in the city, so why wouldn't I make him my manager?"

Dash had started at the name of the theatre, but Blumenthal

didn't notice. The owner of the Pantages, the man with the flashlight. Figures. *Why not make this even harder, Universe?*

"So I paid him twenty percent of my take," Blumenthal continued, "and in the spring, he goes to Farnham for five percent more. Farnham the Farter or whatever he's calling himself these days. A crummy magician is what he is. And don't think Charlie Gluckman is above sending a boy to spy. To take my methods."

"I'm not a spy."

Blumenthal shook his head. "You think you know your friends," he muttered. "Believe me, you don't know your friends."

Dash let him grumble. He looked around the apartment. It was not a very homey place. There were two different chairs in the kitchen and neither of them went with the rickety table. He couldn't be doing very well. Maybe Houdini could really help him. Dash's eye fell on the sugar-coated bun again. "What is that?"

"What?" said Blumenthal, turning his head. "The *rogeleh*? It's a *rogeleh.*"

"*What* is it?"

"It's the last one is what it is." His glance went back and forth between the boy and the pastry, and with a grunt of resignation, he grabbed the plate and held it out to Dash.

"All right, so. This *trick,*" he said, "this magnificent *trick.* What happens in it?"

Dash chewed quickly. The *rogeleh* was even better than the cherry purse. He explained about the vanish and Blumenthal listened with an unimpressed look on his face.

"Easy," said the magician, when he'd finished talking. "Trap door."

"No trap door," said Dash. "The stage was solid underneath me. And I didn't fall through anything. I was still on the stage. And there was *no one in the theatre.*"

Now Blumenthal screwed up his mouth in an odd smile. "I'll give you this, you keep a straight face. Did you hear anything unusual during the trick?"

"No."

"Did you *go* somewhere?"

"Here."

"I mean, when you were still onstage."

Dash shrugged. He couldn't say. He'd been in the dark.

"I could do it if I had some smoke and a trap door."

"No smoke, no trap door," Dash said between bites.

"Look, kid, I gotta walk my squirrel. Whaddaya want from me? You want money?"

"I want to go to Montreal."

"You think I got *that* kind of money?"

"You could come with us."

"*Look.* The *rogeleh* is on the house, and here . . ." He stood up from the table and dug in his pocket. "I got a buck forty-six. But now you should go." He put a handful of coins into Dash's hand. "G'wan. Before I call for a constable and let him decide what happens to ya."

"I think you're my only chance to get home, Mr. Blumenthal! And I think *I* might be your only chance to be great."

But Herman Blumenthal remained unmoved. He held the door open and waited. He wasn't going to change his mind. "Don't take any wooden nickels," he said, sweeping Dash out of his apartment.

11

There was no point in rushing now. There wasn't going to be a train to miss. Dash, his shoulders slumped, turned south on Yonge Street. He was pretty sure Walt was going to be as upset about this turn of events as he was. He passed Richmond, Adelaide, and King streets. The clock on the corner of Yonge and King told him the Montreal train was leaving in twenty minutes.

He turned on Front and there was Union Station. He crossed and went inside. The main floor was exactly as he remembered: a high ornamental ceiling arched over the marble floors of the concourse far below. Walt was inside, waiting near a fruit stand. He had two little rucksacks at his feet.

"Where's Herman Blumenthal?"

"He wouldn't come. I don't think he believes me."

"Sure," said Walt. "I guess you spend all your time trying to trick people, you think everyone's trying to trick you."

"I don't think he likes people very much."

"Great. So now what?"

"I don't know." Over the loudspeakers they were already announcing the train to Montreal.

"Let's see if we can get on it anyway."

"I don't know, Walt. Won't we get caught?"

"Well, we'll have to be careful. They've got rail bulls here."

"Rail bulls?"

"Police. Train police. They hit people who jump on trains with big sticks."

"Oh, well, no big deal, then—"

"You have proof that *we went* to Montreal, Dash. We should at least try to get there."

Dash was scared, but he saw that Walt was right. "Okay. So let's just go straight to the Montreal train and get on it. We'll say, uh . . ."

"We're catching up with our parents. They already showed our tickets."

"Yeah. Good," said Dash, and they started off for the ramp that led into the bowels of the station.

It was dimly lit down here. To get to the platforms, they had to walk under the tracks and they could hear the huge cars rumbling over their heads. They tried to blend into the river of bodies narrowing toward the stairs that led to the Montreal platform.

Once they got there, people jostled to find their cars. The train was packed. A man had asked them for their tickets right away, but they each gestured confidently at the train and told him they'd just gone for candies and their parents were already aboard. He smiled them through, reminding them for next time that there was a restaurant on the train that sold plenty of candy. He wanted to know which car they were in. Three, Dash told him, making it up, and the man pointed them toward it.

"Good news about the restaurant car," Dash said. "Blumenthal gave me a buck forty-six."

"Gimme my quarter!" Walt laughed, but Dash kept the money in his pocket.

Car three was first-class. They straightened their rucksacks on their backs and stood tall. A steward in a very black suit was standing by that door looking at the ticket of a woman in a fur coat.

"Let's go to steerage," said Walter. "Might be easier."

They went back a few cars, but when they tried to convince the steward that their parents were inside car six, he brushed them off. He'd seen train-jumpers before.

So had the stewards at cars eight and eleven.

At the bottom of the stairs, back beneath the tracks, the man who'd let them onto the platform glared at them.

"This sucks," Dash groused. "And before you ask, if something sucks, it's really bad."

"Well, then, I agree that this sucks."

They sagged together on a bench back in the concourse like a pair of sad, old men. The final boarding announcement sounded over their heads.

"Well. At least we have money for a malt," Walt said.

"What's a malt?"

"What's a malt! Come on. An ice cream malt?"

"I don't know what you're talking about."

Walt stood and put his hands on his hips and leaned back. "You'll see. A malt will help us think."

He drew Dash toward a wall of little shops. At the end was Creighton's Soda Shop. A countertop wound a lazy blue S through the middle of it.

Walt took a seat at the counter, dropping the rucksacks beside him. "Two malts," he said to a man in a uniform the same blue as everything else in the shop. He wore a peaked paper hat on his head. Dash watched him crack an egg into each of the big fluted glasses. "Raw eggs?"

"Put hair on your chest," the man called over his shoulder. "Chocolate?"

"Yessir," said Walt. "Now, listen, maybe we should go back out front and try to catch a ride with someone. There could be a bigwig at the Royal York Hotel who wouldn't mind driving two kids to Montreal."

"I don't know about that. My mum and dad always tell me not to get into cars with strangers."

"What stranger? It'd just be a guy with a car."

"I don't think we should."

The drinks arrived. Six cents in total. In each glass, there was a large round ball of chocolate ice cream floating in a mass of fizzing foam. Dash watched Walt navigate his straw around the ice-cream orb and into the creamy, cold liquid below. It was so cold the glasses were sweating.

Walt said, "We could hire a taxi!"

He took a slurp and Dash copied him, sucking in a big mouthful.

"It would cost more than a train," said Dash, "and between the two of us we still only have—" He stopped talking.

"Um, are you okay?"

"What did you say this was again?"

"A malt?"

"It's *incredible!*"

"You really don't have them in 2011?"

"We have milkshakes. Not malts. I don't *think*. Give me a minute." Dash drank slow and deep. It was like drinking a feather pillow, only cold. How, in the advanced, super-connected future, could no one still be making malts?

The station was filling with people again. There was something called the Toronto Railway Line; it seemed to bring people in from smaller towns around the city. A voice boomed out from white hornlike speakers announcing the arrivals and departures:

Streetsville 8:55 arriving on platform two!

Mimico 8:57 arriving on platform six!

Dash sighed, resigned. "What are we going to do, Walt?"

Gravenhurst arriving on platform four!

Crew to loading! Freight track three!

"Hold on!" said Walt, cocking his ear.

Freight track three! Crew to loading!

"We'll get on a train we don't need a ticket for!"

"What are you talking about?"

"They don't ticket freight, Dash. Didn't you hear? There's one loading right now. What if it's going east?"

"Oh . . .!"

"See?" said Walt. "Malts are good for your brain."

They went back under the station and took an unmanned set of stairs up to the platforms again. The freight trains were on tracks beyond the passenger platforms. A couple had open cars piled with wood from front to back, but there were others—squat, windowless cars and silver cars with slits for air. Many of the freight doors were open to the platform, exposing their cargo—crates and bales, machinery and barrels. As they approached one of them, they smelled a warm, earthy scent, and hear the sound of many mouths breathing softly. Cattle and swine.

They tried to walk casually, like they were just curious about the train, and then Walt grabbed a vertical bar at one end of a car and swung himself onto a steel step.

"Come on," he called out to Dash, and he reached for his hand. "There's an opening in this car. Let's see what direction the train heads. We can just jump down if it goes west."

Dash reached out and Walt pulled him up onto the narrow step. "Are you sure about this?"

"You got a better idea?"

They were in a car with special shelving on which were stacked boxes wrapped in butcher paper. It didn't look very comfortable. They walked through it quietly, hunching down past the open doors in the middle of the car. They had to open another door at the end and step out onto the big metal coupling that joined the trains. Even with the cars at a standstill, it felt like a dangerous thing to do.

They crossed gingerly and entered the next car. This one was open to the tracks through a wide central door. It had crates full of apples and pears lined up against the walls, bins as big as washing machines. They crouched against the bins and reached up to grab some of the fruit. Suddenly, one of the pears went flying out of Dash's hand and sailed out the opening: the train had started moving. The two locked eyes.

"East?" asked Dash.

"I'm pretty sure."

They stayed as still as they could. Walt pointed up at one of the huge bins of fruit, but Dash shook his head hard.

"No," he whispered. "We'll be drowned in applesauce by the time we get there. Just stay still."

They sat with their legs crossed and pulled in to keep them from view. The train moved slowly at first. A couple more pieces of fruit they'd moved too close to the bin's edges tipped out and bounced around a little before shooting out the door and backwards. The train was picking up speed.

Dash put an apple to his mouth, but before he could get his teeth in it, Walt was on his feet again with a terrified look on his face.

At the end of the car, standing in the open doorway, was a man in a blue uniform and a cap. He was already reaching for his truncheon.

"Don't move a muscle, you little beggars, if you don't want to feel Billy's sting!"

"Run!" cried Walt. He was already wrenching open the door at the end of the car by the time Dash registered that the rail bull was stalking down the thin space between the crates.

"Wrong decision, lads!" he shouted, and Dash leapt up and ran.

The car ahead, as he saw it through the door, caught the sun redly and seemed to move independently of the car he was still on. That's because it *was* independent. Each car in a train moves over the track freely, the couplings like steel elastic bands, letting the cars shift around. Dash stood at the end of the car looking down at the tracks blurring past. Walt was already on the other side, holding his hand out to him. He felt the sharp sting of the bull's truncheon on his calf and he cried out. A hand clamped onto his shoulder like a vise and the bull spun him around.

"See what happens to train-hoppers, eh?" the man cried, but at that very moment, an apple exploded into green fragments against his forehead. His hands flew to his face and he stumbled backwards, howling.

Clocked by a Granny Smith!

"GIMME YOUR HAND!" Walt cried, and Dash reached out and grabbed it, almost oblivious to the roar behind him, but still very aware of the steel couplers shimmying madly like they were having a thumb war in steel. His teeth felt like they were going to leap out of his head. "Jump!" shouted Walt. "He's getting up!"

Dash leapt with both feet without even touching the couplings and Walt pulled him through the air into the next car. Then both boys were up and running again.

Walt threw open the door at the end of that car and spread his legs between the space to open the next. The bull was through and running toward them. He wasn't speaking anymore, just hollering, and Walt got the door open and pushed across. He didn't have long legs but he was determined not to land in the bull's hands. Dash's calf throbbed, but he followed close behind.

They ran through two more cars, one full of what looked like cabinets, but which Walt said were iceboxes, and then another with canvas bags hanging from big hooks lining the walls.

There was now a car between them and their pursuer.

"This guy's gonna kill us," said Walt. "We have to hide."

"We have to jump."

"Are you kidding? We'll break our necks!"

The sound of hollering came to them from one car away. They went over into the next one and closed the door behind them.

They weren't alone. This was a car with slits along the sides. Inside were kennels. Full of pigs.

"Keep going!" shouted Walt, but Dash was standing in the middle of the car, looking around.

"No," he said. "Get in! Get in a cage!"

"Are you craz—?" Walt began, but already they could hear the door in the car behind opening.

"Look," said Dash. He got an apple out of his pocket and held it in front of one of the cages. A pig snuffled the skin through the bars and tried to scrape at it with its teeth. Dash opened the door and tossed the apple in. "Do it, Walt! Get in!" He ducked down and scuttled quickly behind the pig. The animal moved out of the way. It was more concerned with the apple.

"I'm going to kill you, Dash."

"Kill me later! Here he comes!"

Walt wrenched open the door to the kennel beside Dash's and held out a pear. The animal accepted the fruit with the same porcine eagerness that Dash's had. Walt steeled himself and pushed into the cage behind it, just as the door at the end of the car flew open.

The bull came storming down the middle. He was saying something like "*Argagonnakrackenen!*" and he went all the way down to the end of the car and threw that door open.

A moment later, it slammed shut.

"Ohhh . . ." Walt exhaled in relief. "That was close."

Dash was feeding his pig another apple. "We better stay here."

"In cages with pigs? I'm not going to be lunch!"

"They eat apples, not stringbeans."

"Ha," said Walter, without inflection. Then he began looking around suspiciously. "We'll have to get off at some point. They'll figure out we didn't jump and they'll come back looking."

"You want to try to make a break for it next time the train stops and try to outrun one of these guys on land?"

"I guess not," Walt said.

"How many more apples and pears you got?"

"A few."

"Get busy making friends, then."

The train was picking up speed. A few minutes later, the bull came back through, muttering to himself. He didn't bother checking in the cages, but if he had, all he would have seen was pigs.

A full-grown pig is a like a naked two-hundred-pound baby with thick, bristly hair all over it. In order to hide behind one, or so some people have discovered, it is important to position your body so that at no time will the pig sit on you. This involves soft, cajoling words and a number of apples or pears to establish that you would like to sit *with* the pig and not *under* it.

The really good thing about a full-grown, two-hundred-pound pig is that it is excellent camouflage for a lanky eleven-year-old, and both Dash and Walt fit that description. In fact, they had much time in the six hours it took to get to Montreal to look at each other between the cages, rolling their eyes at their predicament but pleased with their bravery. They realized they could have been mistaken for brothers, both with dark hair, pale skin, and big eyes. Though Dash's eyes were brown; Walter's were blue, just like his sister's.

The pigs were both sows with heavy eyelashes and gentle expressions. They smelled like hay and sweat and poo, in that order, but the boys didn't mind. Just the same, six hours in a steel compartment with a large, sloppy mammal and the cold air whistling through the slits can feel a lot longer, and more than once, Walter reminded Dash that getting into the cages had been *his* idea.

After Kingston, they were so cold that each snuggled up to his host, and after that, it was only a matter of time before their snores rose along with those of the other creatures, who, curled up and lulled by the rocking of the train, had also fallen asleep.

12

Later, Dash would wonder how it must have looked to the people on the platform in the Gare de Montreal.

First they would have seen the train pulling in, the smoke and steam spreading in a long plume against the roof of the station, and then, as it stopped, heard the sounds of animals snuffling the air. Then they were going to get a surprise.

Through the slits, Dash saw passengers waiting on the platforms with stewards, baggage carriers, families and rail police. Plenty of bulls, in fact. Clearly, word had been sent ahead about the stowaways and bulls were watching the doors of the freight trains carefully. And a phalanx of uniformed men stepped down from the nearest platform and crossed the rails, fanning out toward the freight train.

"Last stop," Dash said quietly from inside the car. He and Walt walked backwards, opening the doors to the cages along the floor. "Everybody out."

The train shook as the men mounted the cars in unison.

One of them appeared in the doorway of their car. This will be quite a sight for him, Dash thought as he and Walt paddled the pigs on their bottoms and sent them charging down the aisle in a pink, squealing throng. The man at the other end of the car flew backwards and tumbled from the train, hollering in alarm.

Dash grabbed Walt's arm. "Go! Now!"

They pushed against the flow of the pigs and made their way to the door at the other end of the car. Dash opened it a crack and saw more men coming. But their eyes were on the mayhem, not the space between the cars, and Dash slid out like a shadow and quickly disappeared behind the next car. Walt shut the door and slid away as well, joining Dash behind the commotion.

They stood utterly still, not daring to breathe. Pigs thundered toward the passenger platforms. On the faces of the travellers awaiting their train on the last platform before the yard, Dash saw a mixture of amusement and the dawning realization that they'd have to get out of the way.

"Go, pigs," said Walt quietly.

"You mean, *thanks*, pigs! We're here! We better move it: the clock at the end of that platform says it's almost eight o'clock. Houdini's going to be done soon!"

They waited a few moments longer, as the clattering of footsteps and the sound of whistles grew quieter. Then they ran, crouching periodically, to the end of the train, and out in front of it, making a mad dash for the safety of the crowds. They immediately slowed to a walk and melted into them. From there it was nothing to vanish into the flashing, honking, hooting, clamouring streets of Montreal at 8 p.m. on a Wednesday night in 1926.

Walt's face was caked with dirt. "That was . . . amazing," he said. "I don't even think they saw us." He exhaled a long breath and laughed with relief. "Never a dull moment with you, Dash— Holy . . . *pig*! Look at that!"

A pig was running up the street, twisting in and out of traffic. "We better keep moving," Dash said. "We have a lecture to catch . . ."

They made their way to the main road: it was called Rue Sainte-Catherine and it was a zoo up here, and not just because of the pigs. The sidewalks were crazy with people—people walking dogs; women in fine hats walking arm-in-arm with men, with other women, sometimes alone; children walking with their parents; old people taking the air. It seemed that everyone was smoking. The doors to the bars swung open and shut. Such noise! Such life!

Dash had never visited Montreal, so he had no idea how different this might be from Montreal in the *real* present. But if the Montreal of his time bore any relation to the one in 1926, then it was quite the place. As they walked along the busy avenue, those black-hooded Fords were everywhere, parping their horns, pulling over to curbs, pulling away from curbs, like it was a game of musical cars. Men leaned out the windows of parked cars, arms draped over their steering wheels, talking animatedly to people on the sidewalk. It was a party everyone was invited to, a hoot. Hopefully someone in the madness could tell them where McGill University was.

"Wipe your face!" Dash said to Walt. "You're filthy."

"You are too."

They ran their hands over their cheeks and picked the tufts of hay out of their hair.

It turned out *everyone* knew where McGill University was, only everyone had a different idea about how to get there. Dash and Walt decided the best route was to follow the brightly lit main road. A mist had come into the air, and the boys walked along Sainte-Catherine with their heads lowered, trying not to attract attention.

Soon, they came to McGill College Avenue, wide and straight, and as they turned onto it, they saw the gates of the university ahead of them, lamps on either side casting a warm glow through the haze. Some people were entering those gates, but the avenue was much calmer than the main street had been.

Up at the gates, they saw a big poster that said:

WEDNESDAY ONLY
HARRY HOUDINI
WILL ADDRESS THE McGILL COMMUNITY ON THE ILLS OF SPIRITUALISM
THE FAMED MAGICIAN

**THROUGH DEMONSTRATION AND DISCUSSION
WILL DEBUNK ALL THE CLAIMS OF SPIRIT MEDIUMS**

6:30 p.m.
McGILL STUDENT UNION BALLROOM
ADMISSION FREE

It was already eight fifteen.

"Geez!" said Dash. "We've probably missed it!"

They ran up through the centre of campus, big stone buildings looming in the mist, and hunted frantically for the Student Union. When they got there, the doors were already closed, locked from the outside.

They stood on the steps and looked around. It was quiet here. Walter tried the door again and Dash searched for another way in around the side. A man walking by with a cane came out of a passageway.

"You boys lost?" he asked Dash.

"No," said Dash. "We're fine."

"Houdini's in there tonight," the man said.

"Yeah, we know. But we can't get in."

"Try the back door," the man said, pointing with his cane. He had a white, walrus-y moustache under his nose.

"There's a back door?" said Dash. "Thanks!"

"Who you talking to?" asked Walt, coming to where Dash was.

"This man says—" started Dash, but the man was gone. "There's a back door."

They ran around the side of the building, where they could

hear laughter and then applause through the brick wall. There was a steel door propped open with a tin can full of sand and cigarette butts. They slipped inside, and saw people standing in the hallway, trying to listen through the open doors to the lounge. The boys crept past them and down a side hall and began trying the doors. One opened and they walked through into a wall of black suits. Men and women were standing three or four deep around the edges of the room.

"This is where we're standing in the picture!" Walter said into Dash's ear.

"Move up!" said Dash.

Walt pushed through the men, excusing himself. The sea of tall, thin bodies parted, and they reached the middle of the crowd. Dash followed, whispering his apologies, and then there was a flash of light and he realized they'd gotten there in the nick of time. The man with the camera had just taken the picture. Dash saw him standing on the other side of the cramped lounge.

Unless, thought Dash, he *couldn't* take the picture *until* they had arrived. He still wasn't sure how this worked. Had he already *been* here? If someone could give him a picture of himself in his time that had been *taken* in 1926, then he must have been here already. He'd been here then and he was here now. Although, how could any of that be? He shook his head, confounded, and then he heard the voice. He lifted his eyes and saw he was ten feet from Harry Houdini.

The great man was sitting in a plain wooden chair at the

front of the room, and speaking in a strong American accent. He was saying,

"Do we stand idly by while the credulous and the lonesome are feasted upon? The practice of spiritualism is getting to be a very serious thing! The truth should be established beyond a shadow of a doubt, by undeniable evidence. I will tell you this, my friends: in thirty-five years, I have never seen one genuine medium. Millions of dollars are stolen every year by spiritualists, from people who are struck by grief, or living in foolish hope, and governments will do nothing about it because they consider it a religion!"

There was appreciative applause, which extended itself when Houdini stood and took his bows. His right ankle was bandaged above the top of his shoe. Dash remembered that Houdini had broken it earlier that month in Albany, New York, performing his Water Torture Cell.

"Now, if you'd like some *rational* entertainment," he said, "I propose a performance that will nonetheless bring you to the brink of believing in spirits again. I will be performing at the Princess Theatre tonight through Saturday afternoon. I promise you an experience of great mystification and delight." And with a flourish, Houdini walked out a door at the back of the room. He was limping, but he held his head high.

"Come on!" said Dash. "We have to talk to him."

"Wait," said Walt, as black forms moved around them, lighting their cigarettes. Like crows wreathed in clouds of smoke. "Whadder we gonna say to him?"

"I don't know!" Dash led the way back out into the Union's hallways, away from the crowd. "I might have to tell him the truth."

"That should work like a charm."

"Well, what am I supposed to do?"

"I don't know, maybe—"

"Where are you boys going?"

A large blue chest had materialized in front of them. A guard with a ruddy face and hands the size of catcher's mitts. Both boys tracked their eyes up the barrel chest to the large, dark eyes.

"We, uh, we have to tell Houdini something," said Dash. "It's important."

"I'm sure he doesn't need to hear from the likes of you. What are you doing back here, anyway?"

"We came to hear him speak," said Dash. "We're fans."

"Fans?" said the guard.

"Our mother died because of a spiritualist!" Walt burst out. "A lady spiritualist just down on Sainte-Catherine told 'er that she had to get 'er *charms* every week. An', an', an' . . . ." He was running out of material and looking over at Dash. He hid his face in his arm and pretended to cry.

Dash continued. "Never mind him, sir. I understand you gotta protect Mr. Houdini. He's a famous person! It's just this lady spiritualist took all our money and then Mum, well . . . *she ran away*! And Mr. Houdini was talking this very night about that same lady who destroyed our family, and we just wanna thank him is all."

The guard was staring at them, stonelike, impassive. His eyes twitched back and forth between Dash's face and the top of Walt's sobbing head. "What a loada malarky, pure and simple," he said. Then he stood aside. "*G'wan*. Go to the end of the hall and see the other guard. Tell him Erich is expecting you. He'll let you pass."

The two of them sprung forward. The hall outside the lounge was getting busier. They came to the guard at the end.

"We're here to see Erich," they said at the same time.

"Calm down, gentlemen! He's the third door on the right. Knock and wait to be invited in."

"We will!" They took urgent strides to the third door on the right.

"Before you knock," Walt said, grabbing Dash's wrist. "Do I look okay?"

"What?"

"I'm meeting *Houdini*!"

"Dude, you're fine."

"You think he'll help us?"

"I dunno," Dash said. "*Someone* has to help us! We sure can't count on Blumenthal."

That's when a voice said, "Blumenthal?" They hadn't noticed the dressing room door was standing open. "Who's Blumenthal?" said a man in a black suit with a vest. There was a gold chain strung between two pockets.

"Sol?" came a voice from deeper within. "Who is it?"

"Two boys," said the man. "Gossiping."

"Excellent," said the voice. "Invite them in."

13

The man named Sol pulled the door open to reveal Houdini sitting in his shirtsleeves before a small mirror and a table. He had been reading a couple of letters that lay open in front of him. There was one other man in the room, dressed in a long grey overcoat. His shoes were rattier than most Dash had seen. He smiled unkindly at them when they entered the room.

"Um," said Dash. "Hello."

"Come in, come in," said Houdini. "Would you boys like some autographs?"

The door closed behind them. It was like someone's furnace room, and the air in it was tight with smoke. Houdini was the only one who *wasn't* smoking. His face appeared like it was in its own light. This close up, even closer than he'd been to them in the lounge, Houdini seemed to Dash more miraculously alive. He had an intelligent, catlike face, and brown, glowing eyes. There was a little grey in his hair, hair that lay in tight waves against his head.

"Are you two brothers?" he asked.

"No, sir," said Dash. "He's Walter Gibson, my friend."

"And your name?"

"Dashiel Woolf."

"I see." Houdini looked up at Sol and raised an eyebrow. He stood and offered his hand to Walt first. "Is your name really Walter Gibson?"

"Yes." He shook the man's hand in grinning stupefaction.

"That is the name of a very good friend of mine, you know."

"Is it?"

"And you, do they call you Dash for short?"

"Yes, sir."

He smiled at them. "Well, that was my brother Theo's nickname. From his Hungarian name Ferencz Dezso. We called him Dash."

"That is . . . very interesting, sir. And Walt here having your friend's—"

"Are those your real names?" asked the third man. He had deep-set eyes inside a blocky, rectangular face.

"Our real—Oh yes, sir, yes!" said Dash. "I don't know Mr. Houdini's brother's name, honestly! And he *is* Walter Gibson. I've met his parents. That's what they call him."

Houdini frowned. "Do your parents actually call you 'Walter Gibson,' Walter Gibson?"

"They call me Walt, sir."

"Well, *Walt*," said the third man. "Say your piece and make like an egg—*scramble*." He laughed at his joke and then looked anxiously at his host.

"Oh, Gordon," said Houdini, "I've just thought of a book I'd like to lend you."

"Yes, Harry. What is it? I'd be very interested to know the book you are thinking of."

"It's a biography of the great magician and snake-oil salesman, Katterfelto. Would you come by my hotel later and pick it up, perhaps? I'm at the Mont Royal."

"Well, yes, I believe I could do that."

"What time later tonight would suit you? Say ten o'clock?"

The man called Gordon considered this for a moment. "Well," he said at last, "I believe I could make it around then."

"Excellent," said Houdini, rising and limping past the boys to the door. "I look forward to it."

Gordon lurched out of his seat. He was being excused. His face looked panicked for a moment and then he reassembled it. He tugged his coat straight and touched the tip of his cap as he went past. "Well, I will try to make it, Harry. And I do, yes, I rather look forward to explaining my personal method in more detail, as you so kindly suggest."

"Thank you again." Houdini closed the door silently on Gordon. He whispered something in Sol's ear.

"I'm Sol Jacobson," the man said to the boys, smiling kindly. He wore a grey fedora like no other person Dash had ever seen, like he must have been born wearing it. There was a hand-rolled cigarette burning in the corner of his mouth.

"Hello, Mr. Jacobson."

He gestured to a seat. "Let us get to know one another. I am Harry's manager. And his friend. Are you friends?"

The boys looked at each other, and without hesitation they both said, "Yes," although Walt said it first.

"Well, then," said Sol Jacobson, "you will understand it is my job to protect Harry from silly things, shenanigans, little tricksters. And just, you know, look at him—" He looked over at Houdini fondly and Houdini batted his eyes. "He is a wee slip of a man with a fragile constitution."

"Oh, stop it now," said Houdini. "Let them say their piece. You have a piece, don't you, gentlemen? I can feel it."

"Go directly to the truth," said Jacobson, "*Dash* and *Walter*."

"Well, sir, you see," began Dash, "I'm kind of in trouble, and I thought maybe you might be able to help me."

Jacobson's face took on a hard set. "This wouldn't be a request for money, would it?"

"Just *show* him," said Walt, barely moving his mouth.

"Show me what?" asked Houdini, and he was perhaps one percent less friendly in his tone. "What have you got?"

Dash stood up and took the newspaper clipping out of its envelope. He unfolded it and put it picture-side up in Houdini's palm. Houdini read down the first column. Then he studied the photograph.

"That was five minutes ago," said Dash.

Houdini blinked. "I see," he said. "Interesting. Where did you get this?"

"It was given to me."

"By whom?"

"A boy. Not him," he said, gesturing at Walter. "Another boy."

"And where did *he* get it?"

"I don't know," said Dash.

Jacobson took the paper from Houdini and looked at it carefully, turning it over in his hands. "Harry" he said, "where is that tie you wore tonight?"

"On the divan." He accepted the paper back, and Jacobson went to get Houdini's tie. It was dark blue with silvery stars scattered over it.

"You wear this tie frequently enough at your lectures, Harry. Anyone could have done a clever mock-up."

"The paper looks very old. It smells old."

"One week in a teapot will do that."

Houdini had not taken his eyes off of the boys. "Let them remove their jackets, perhaps."

Jacobson hesitated, but then he held his hand out for their suit jackets. "You have three minutes," he said.

"Two," said Houdini, studying the newspaper clipping. "Or perhaps just one." He handed it back to Dash. "That's quite an excellent fraud."

"Fraud?"

"Well, Sol is correct. I've given this lecture many times before, so the type for the story could have been set in advance. What with darkroom advances these days, it's entirely possible someone could have taken that photograph within the last two hours and had a good counterfeit made up in time. It's very clever, I warrant. But even so, that *is* the tie I wore tonight . . . and I think I see the bottom of the banner that was hanging at the back of the room. Very clever indeed."

Dash said, "This newspaper is eighty-five years old."

Houdini seemed to be looking over Jacobson's shoulder at a spot on the wall. "A mist of water," he said with a distracted air, "a few coffee grounds, a little grubbing and an iron."

"It's not fake. That is us—Walter and I—in the picture."

"Walter and *me*."

"Yes, sir."

"So be it, then," said Jacobson, interrupting. "You say it's real, but *I* say it's suppertime, and not too early for a rye. And we have"—he looked at his watch—"exactly one hour before Bess comes looking for you."

"Oh, let them say what they've come for first."

"I vote for beefsteak," said Jacobson.

"We've heard most of it, I'm sure." Houdini returned his attention to them. "Are you selling this? It's a short-lived trick, though, isn't it? The *Gazette* will come out in the morning and prove it."

"It *will* prove it. This is tomorrow's paper, the day before it comes out."

"All right, then, well done. Do you want a dollar for it?"

"No!" said Dash. "I don't want money."

"Then what do you want?" asked Houdini. "Applause?"

"Someone gave me this newspaper clipping. In 2011."

"Two thousand eleven what?"

"Years. The *year* 2011. Eighty-five years from now, someone gave me this newspaper and then I was in a magic trick that went wrong. And I ended up *here*, in 1926, and found *him* walking down the street in Toronto. And he's *in* the picture. *Look*."

The magician looked warily where Dash had placed his finger.

"And that cufflink? It's mine. Look, I'm wearing them right now. I was wearing them when I left my house."

"In 2011."

"Right."

Jacobson, who had sat for Dash's speech, now stood again, slapping his legs. "Well! It sounds like a matter for science, doesn't it?"

"Yes," said Houdini, collecting his things. "Thank you very much for your visit."

"No!" cried Dash.

"You two can come with me," said Jacobson. He went out the door expecting them to follow, but neither boy budged.

"We stowed away in a train fulla pigs and hid from the police to get here!" Walter said in a heated tone. "We came from Toronto. We don't have anything to eat or anywhere to sleep."

"So you are *fanatics*, then," said Houdini with distaste.

"Mr. Houdini," said Dash, "I know you just told all those people to be careful about spiritualists and people *like* them—"

Houdini's eyes darkened. "And?"

"And, well, I'm sure you're right! But, but . . . what if there are *other* things, things you *can't* understand—"

"I am mainly interested in what I *can* understand, Master Woolf, but I am in the business of mystifying others, and I can tell the difference between an enigma and a sham. Now, if you boys will excuse me—"

Dash felt his jaw trembling. "I thought you were the greatest magician who ever lived!"

"What has that to do with anything?" asked Jacobson, standing in the doorway again.

"I thought he would help me!"

"Oh, pish-tosh. No one is falling for this."

Dash turned on Jacobson, seething. "And if you were really his friend, you'd get him to listen!"

"I *am* his friend," said Jacobson, "and I am getting him to *dinner*."

"Come on!" Dash said to Walter. "Let's go."

They got up to leave, but Houdini stopped them. "Where are your parents?"

"Mine are in Toronto," said Walter.

"So are mine," said Dash. "In 2011. In a *theatre*. Waiting for me to be *un*vanished. EXCEPT I'M STUCK HERE IN 1926!"

"Oh for goodness' sake—fine," Houdini said. "Sol, perhaps you could locate the man who was authorized to take pictures this evening and have him come to my hotel in one hour."

"Which one?"

"The Prince of Wales. I keep two hotels in every city," he said to the boys. He pulled his suit jacket on. "Are you really runaways?"

"Walter's parents don't actually know where he is right now. They think he's having a sleepover."

"And yours? Where are they, really?" Dash didn't reply. "All right, get them some supper," he said to Jacobson. "And I believe I will have a walk and a think before coming back. Does the hotel have a telephone for public use?"

"I believe they do. And I will also make sure Gordon Whitehead receives a couple of books at the front desk at the Mont Royal, with your regrets that you are unable to meet him." He gave a little bow.

Houdini steepled his fingertips under his chin, like an Asiatic king.

Jacobson showed the boys out. There was one of those Fords waiting for them in the curving driveway in front of the Student Union. Jacobson got into the passenger seat beside a driver wearing thick glasses and a cap. Jacobson said the name of the hotel and then the car started off. It was a much more comfortable mode of transport than hiding behind pigs.

Jacobson turned in his seat and looked at his guests. He wore a not unfriendly look. But it wasn't friendly either. "So. A rather long trip, then."

"Yes," Dash said.

"Harrowing, one would say."

"Yes."

"And I suppose I will have to call your parents, Master Gibson. What am I to tell them?"

"I left them a note saying I had a sleepover."

"That is bound to fall apart. Better tell them something they can believe that's closer to the truth."

"That we were kidnapped?"

Jacobson narrowed his eyes severely. "I don't suppose your parents have a telephone, do they?"

"They're on a trunk line."

"All right. You had better leave this to me."

14

In a matter of minutes, driving straight along Sainte-Catherine, they arrived at the Prince of Wales Hotel. It was an unprepossessing building, just a couple of stories high and made of solid grey stone. There was a bar on the corner.

Inside, it was quietly luxurious, and Jacobson took the two of them into the restaurant behind the bar, a small, velvety room redolent of roasted meat. It was past nine now, but the restaurant was packed and loud. Jacobson spoke to the maître d'—*Marcel*, he called him—and the boys were shown to a cozy banquette with leather seats. The way the booth was curved meant they'd be sitting side by side, watching the activity in the busy room.

The man who brought them to the table swept a napkin off Dash's plate, opened it with a neat flip of the wrist, and settled it on his lap, then repeated the performance for Walt. Around the shining white plates was arrayed a bewildering assortment of cutlery. Forks of every size, some with only three tines, many delicate-looking spoons as well as a very large one, and a strange-looking pair of tongs with big square flat heads at the ends, like a pair of silver playing cards.

Jacobson came over and sat, and Marcel reappeared with a telephone on a silver tray, like he was going to serve it as an appetizer. A waiter appeared pulling a long, black wire, and he plugged it into the phone. It was quite a production, and everyone in the restaurant had stopped eating to watch it.

"Monsieur will make a telephone call?"

"It's a Toronto number," said Jacobson.

"It can be done."

Walt told Marcel his phone number: HO 3276.

"*Bonjour, mademoiselle*," the maître d' sang into the receiver. He held it in front of his mouth like a microphone. "*Comment allez-vous ce soir? Bien, merci! Donc, Toronto, s'il vous plaît. Oui: ash–oh, trente-deux, soixante-seize.*" He waited a moment before passing the phone set to Jacobson.

Jacobson put it up against his ear. They could hear the phone ringing through the receiver.

"Yes," he said. "May I speak to Mrs. Gibson?" He held the earpiece away from his head. There were some fierce clicking noises. Then a voice came on and said a tinny hello. "Yes, hello, Mrs. Gibson," he continued. "Good evening to you. My name is Sol Jacobson and I am calling you on a telephone from inside the Prince of Wales Hotel in Montreal. Yes, Montreal, Canada. Why, yes, it is an excellent connection. I am Mr. Harry Houdini's Canadian manager. Yes, *that* Harry Houdini, madame. I am calling because I am here in Montreal with your son. He is very well, there is no need to be worried. No, madame, he is not at a sleepover, he was involved in a harmless mix-up earlier today and found himself, quite unexpectedly, on a train. Yes, a train to Montreal. He is with me right now. Well, the way he explained it, he and one of his friends went down to the train station at lunchtime. Yes, Union Station. They were trying to make some pennies by helping people with their bags."

Walt gave Dash a wide-eyed look.

"Yes. And you see, they were helping some old dear with her bag, you know, up the steps and into the compartment, when the train began to leave the station. And they were terrified to jump, so . . . yes, I know, absolutely. You can never take your eyes off them. Just the same, quite enterprising, don't you think? Admirable. Harry and I thought they showed some fine initiative, not to mention some good sense staying safe on the train until they could find some adult help." They heard Mrs. Gibson talking on the other end. "Well, Mrs. Gibson, you are quite correct. It was lucky that I ran into them. And I will have them out on the next one. However, I must tell you, there are no more trains for Toronto this evening, and so I will, with your permission, keep them at Harry's hotel until we are able to get them homeward bound. And he has suggested, I should say, that they even stay for one of his shows, seeing as they've come this far."

Both boys were watching Jacobson with wonder.

He passed the phone to Walt. "You'd better talk to her."

"Hi, Mum," he said into the phone. "Yes. I'm very sorry! Yes, a little." Dash heard a muted voice from the other end. "I know," said Walt. "I don't know what I was thinking either. I will. I don't know. He looks like his pictures, I guess." Then he said, very quietly, "I love you too." He handed the phone back to Jacobson.

"Well, then," Jacobson said into the phone, "that settles it. You can reach us here at the Prince of Wales Hotel if you need to. Yes, thank you, Mrs. Gibson. Beg pardon? Oh, well, I can administer that if you feel it's necessary. I'm sure it won't be a problem. Goodbye, then. Goodbye." He gestured for Marcel to come get the phone. The maître d' bustled over and carried the apparatus away.

"Thank you for doing that," Walt said.

"If you are going to the trouble to make something up, gentlemen, at least put some effort into it."

"Are we really going to see the show?" Dash asked.

"Perhaps. If you are not a pair of con men."

"We're not!"

Jacobson stood and put his hat on. "I will leave you two to your suppers," he said. "You're in rather far now, aren't you?"

"Yes," said Dash. He couldn't meet Jacobson's eyes as he left the table. He exhaled deeply. "Are you in a lot of trouble?" he asked Walt.

"What do you think?"

"Grounded for the rest of your life."

Walt laughed. "Well, at least I get to say I met Harry Houdini!"

Dash saw a flurry of activity over by the maître d's desk. He expected to see Houdini entering, but it was a man having a disagreement with the manager. He was wearing a dark blue suit.

"I bet you don't know any French," Dash said.

"Everyone speaks English."

"*Pas içi*," Dash said.

"Gentlemen," said a voice, and they looked up to see the man in the blue suit. He was smiling at them strangely. "Good evening."

"Um, good evening," they said.

The man moved his face into the light. There was a deep, black and purple bruise on his forehead, above his left eye. Apple-sized. "And how are we tonight?"

"We're, um, just *fine*," Dash said, quaking. The man's smile widened. "Just waiting for, uh, our father to get back from the washroom."

"What, two runaways like you, looking for your father?" He came around and shoved into the banquette beside Walt.

Walt jolted over and so did Dash, but the bull just kept coming. Soon he was sitting in the middle, like it was his table.

"Hid with the pigs, did we? Nice scene you made in the *gare*, eh? Heard all about it." He reached into a pocket and removed a green apple, which he began to polish on his lapel.

There was no point in making a run for it. There were already some other, more official-looking people standing in the door. One of them had a clipboard: a lady with a severe face and broad shoulders.

"I'll introduce you to my friends momentarily," he said, "but first I'd like to know your names." He leered when he said this, and then took a large bite of the apple.

Walt held a hand to his chest. "I am Cornelius, and this is my brother, Vincenzo."

"Born in different countries or something, eh? What are your *real* names?"

"Dash," Dash said, feeling defeated. Was anything going to go right? "And he's Walter."

"Excellent," said the bull. "My name is Blackwell. Sometimes people call me Officer Blackwell, but seeing as I am in civilian togs, you can just call me Sir. Being off duty, I am just like any other member of the general public, out to take the evening air, say, and being a member of the general public, I may alert authorities—for instance, as a good citizen—to the fact that there are two homeless boys at large in the dangerous metropolis of Montreal. Luckily, the city is replete with excellent services for travellers in need." He gestured to the entrance of the restaurant. "Why, look, there is Mrs. Alphonsine of the Children's Welfare Bureau. She cannot stand to see children suffer."

"We're not suffering," Dash said.

"No," said Blackwell, and his eyes lit up. "Not yet."

He gestured to the lady in the stiff black dress and she approached. There were two men with her, large men with moustaches and wearing plain-looking light grey suits. In 1926, it seemed bad news always arrived wearing a moustache.

"I see it is suppertime in Gomorrah," Mrs. Alphonsine said, arriving at the table. "What are these two boys doing in this awful place?"

"Waiting for our father!" Dash protested. Where was Houdini? Where was Jacobson?

Marcel scurried over. "*Madame?*" he said. "*Qu'est-ce qui se passe?*"

She explained to him in French. Dash picked up enough of what she said to understand that they were accused of committing a number of offences and insults against the Canadian National Rail Company. Mr. Blackwell was clearly relishing his triumph.

"*Mais, ils sont avec Monsieur 'Oudini!*" said Marcel.

"No, they are not," Mrs. Alphonsine now said in English. "They are not *with* Houdini. They are not *with* anyone. They stole away on a freight train and attacked an officer of the law."

Marcel looked from her to the boys and back to her again, and then his mouth turned down deeply and his shoulders came up. "I don't know," he said. "I try to 'elp you boys, but if 'Oudini is not here to say is okay, I don't know."

"Please, Marcel!" Dash pleaded. "You know we're his guests!"

"Come now, boys," said one of Mrs. Alphonsine's men. Were they twins? Frick and Frack. "We'll sort it out later."

Blackwell took another bite of his apple and chewed it with pleasure.

Each man held a boy against his side and began to march them out after Mrs. Alphonsine. Dash knew, somehow, it wasn't going to end like this. Houdini was supposed to help him. That was the only thing that made sense. Why else were they here?

It was with a sinking feeling that he saw the man himself

enter the hotel lobby just as Frick and Frack were going to haul them onto the sidewalk.

"Dad!" Walt shouted.

Houdini looked surprised, but for only a moment. "Boys?" he said, with animated alarm. "What have you done now?"

Everyone met in the middle of the lobby. "These children are with me," said Mrs. Alphonsine. "They are runaways."

"No they are not!" said Houdini, flashing with anger. "They are to go to their room immediately to await punishment for whatever rabble they caused in here. I will see to it!"

"Constable Blackwell here insists they are train-hoppers." She gestured to the restaurant behind, where Blackwell had remained. "All will be well. The province will know what to do with them."

"Madame, if I may," said Houdini, "Constable Blackwell is my brother. We had a disagreement about whether my sons here should visit their sick nanny and he felt, well, Terrence felt it would be too much for the old thing and he got a little hot under the collar. You know what it is like in times of family crisis! Ah, here is their other uncle, Sol. Hello, Uncle Sol!"

Jacobson stepped into his role without hesitation. "Hello . . . Harry, dear Harry. How are you, my nephews?"

"We're fine," said Dash. The men had not let go of them yet.

Houdini gave a warm, expectant look at the two burly guards, who at last released the boys. Dash and Walter rushed over to their rescuers, and Houdini pressed them both against Jacobson.

"Take them in to dinner, Uncle Sol. Make sure to let my brother know I've got everything under control." He had not taken his eyes off Mrs. Alphonsine.

Jacobson led them into the restaurant and Marcel seated the three of them at a banquette on the other side of the dining room. The look on Officer Blackwell's face was priceless.

15

Houdini was in the mood for fish. The waiter—Honoré—came to the table with four shallow, empty bowls. He set them down. There was a second man behind him holding a black cauldron on a silver tray. When he lowered it before them, he removed the lid and a plume of fragrant steam rushed up.

"*La . . . bouillabaisse*," said Honoré, fairly bowing to the cauldron.

"Fish soup," said Houdini. "It's excellent here."

Honoré had produced a ladle from somewhere on his person and was filling the bowls. Walter blanched. Dash didn't mind fish, but he wasn't too excited about what was coming out of the cauldron. All he could see were shells and antennae. It was the most frightening thing he had ever seen in a bowl. Once all the fish was served, the second waiter ladled from the cauldron a dark broth.

"*Bon . . . APPÉTIT!*" said Honoré, and both he and the cauldron-bearer backed away, all the way to the kitchen.

"*How* many tickets?" Jacobson was asking.

"I told her to bring the ten best-behaved children to the matinee on Saturday. She talked me up from three."

"We don't have ten seats, Harry. The matinee is sold out."

"We will make room. You boys will come too, if you wish."

"They will be well gone by then, Harry."

Walt was looking into a clam. "How do you eat this?"

"With relish," said Houdini. He sipped a spoonful of soup. "I hear we spoke with your mother, Master Gibson."

"We did," Walter said, almost inaudibly.

"But not yours," he said, turning to Dash.

"No, sir."

"Because . . . she is somewhere in the future, waiting for a magic trick to end."

"Yes, sir."

"How perplexing."

"You believe me?"

"No. I do not. But as you can see, two boys on a fool's errand can end up with the wrong accommodation, if they're not careful. Once we *find* your mother, Master Woolf, we will send you both home. But first, I would like you to meet someone."

Houdini looked across the room to the bar. He gestured to a man who was sitting there drinking a beer. The man was shabbily dressed and had two cameras hanging off one shoulder. On the other shoulder was a green burlap bag. He got up and walked over. Houdini watched his guests' faces carefully as the man approached. Dash felt relieved that at least he would be able to ignore his soup a while longer.

"Mr. Hopkins," Houdini said, standing, "I trust you know these two fellows." He gestured at Dash and Walter.

"I beg pardon, sir? There are three fellows here."

"Yes, that is Sol Jacobson, my manager. I meant these two young men here."

"Hello," Hopkins said, nodding curtly to them. "How do you do."

"I see," said Houdini. "So you don't know these boys?"

"No, sir. Are they to be a part of your act?"

Houdini shot them a glance. "I think they would like to be. Will you have a seat?"

The photographer slid into the end of the banquette. He appeared quite eager to be a part of the company. Honoré drifted to the table and looked into the boys' bowls. He pursed his lips in disappointment.

"Ees to be eaten 'ot!" he said, pushing each of their meals toward them. "And soon are coming the *escargots*."

"Excellent," said Houdini, and sent the waiter off.

The boys had no choice. Dash ate a hunk of white fish, and Walt bit the back half of a shrimp that still had its head.

"You take the shell off," Dash muttered to him as Walt crunched it in his teeth uncomfortably.

"So, Mr. Hopkins. What is your first name?"

"Gerard."

"Ah. And you look so like a Gerard."

"People say that."

"I do think people often look like their first names. For

instance, these boys look very much like their names. Take this one," he said, indicating Walt, "would you say his name was Walter or Gabriel?"

"Oh, that's a Walt if I ever saw one," said Hopkins.

"That is correct! And this one? Calvin or John?"

"John," said Hopkins without hesitation.

"See?" said Houdini to his manager. He was holding down Dash's foot with his own. "He really doesn't know these young men."

"Well, sir, Mr. Houdini, I was dropped on my head when I was a baby, so my memory isn't—"

"That's all right. Master Woolf, could I see that newspaper page again?"

Dash retrieved it. Houdini unfolded it to the picture of himself onstage and passed it over to Mr. Hopkins, who studied the image.

After a moment, the photographer said, "Are you asking my opinion? I think the subject is well lit, and the photograph, as it appears here, is crisp and very legible, although it is only half a picture and of course I would have to—"

"Is that what you think? It is a good photograph?"

"Yes. Is there something wrong with it? Who took it?"

Honoré arrived again. His busboy cleared the bowls as a third man came with a trolley. Honoré looked with disapproval at the two half-finished bowls of bouillabaisse that were whisked away from the boys.

"I 'ope you will find the *escargots* more to your likings, *messieurs*."

He apportioned four strange ceramic plates around the table. They were white plates with little divots in them. The divots were filled with something green from which thick steam rose.

"What are these?" asked Walt with real fear in his voice. Suddenly he sneezed.

"Snails," said Jacobson, leaning away from him. "A treat. Enjoy them."

Houdini continued. "I will tell you who took this picture, Mr. Hopkins. You did. This is *your* photograph. Supposedly you took this picture, less than two hours ago, and it is already in the newspaper. A newspaper, mind you, that is dated tomorrow morning."

Hopkins had been eyeing the *escargots* with interest, but now he studied the picture anew. He took his glasses off and brought the paper up close to his right eye, closing his left. Then he sniffed it. After a long pause, in which he fitted his glasses back over his ears and laid the paper on the table, he said, "That's very good, Mr. Houdini . . . absolutely excellent. Bravo!"

"Do call me Harry. Was there any other photographer backstage with you?"

"No."

"So this *could* be your photograph, then?"

"Well . . . no, sir, no, it could not."

"No?"

"Impossible. The pictures I took at the Student Union are still in my camera. This one, in fact." He held the camera up.

"Eat your snails," Houdini said sharply to Walt.

Dash had already moved some of the green paste with his fork. Underneath were snails. Undeniably. They were still *inside their shells*. Cooked! And stuffed, it would seem, with boiled snot.

"Do you like *escargots*, Mr. Hopkins?" Dash asked.

"Oh, I love them," said the photographer.

Dash hurriedly pushed his plate over. Walt glared.

"Thank you, Mr. Hopkins," said Houdini. "I think that will be all."

Mr. Hopkins paused with a snail shell midway between his plate and his mouth. Then he put it down with a grateful smile, pushed his chair back, and touched his fingers to his cap. "Well. It was a great pleasure to make your acquaintance, Mr. Houdini."

He departed, nodding and bowing left and right.

"I am now officially listening, Master Woolf." Houdini slid the snails back in front of him. "But you had better impress me, or you will be eating both bowls."

16

Harry Houdini listened patiently to Dash's story. For his part, Dash tried to keep his voice calm and his mind focused. At times Houdini looked amused, even charmed.

"And where is Master Gibson from? I mean, what year?"

"What year?" said Walt, offended. "I'm from now! Mr. Jacobson just called my mother!"

"Are you crying, young man?" asked Jacobson.

"No," said Walt. "I'm allergic to fish probably!" He sneezed again, and Jacobson wrinkled his lip and passed him a napkin.

"So then," said Houdini, "the two of you settled on a mission to come and see me in Montreal?"

"Yes," said Dash. "To ask for your help."

"Well, I can get out of a milk jug, but I don't do time travel, gentlemen. As far as I know, no one does. The apparatus is too large to get onstage."

"The apparatus?" asked Walter.

"He means time," said Dash.

Houdini broke off a small piece of bread, put it in his mouth, and chewed thoughtfully before swallowing. "And who is Blumenthal?" he asked.

Dash's eyes went wide. "You know Blumenthal?"

"Sol said you were arguing about a man named Blumenthal outside of my dressing room last night."

"He's the reason we're here! He's the one who invented the trick that went wrong in 2011, although I can't see how that guy—"

"Yeah, *that* guy," echoed Walt.

"Anyway, his *grandson* was performing it when I—"

"When you were sent back in time."

"Yes."

"Well, that seems fairly straightforward then, doesn't it? Just get Blumenthal to do the trick again."

Dash lowered his eyes. "I already thought of that," he said. "But he can't."

"Why?"

"Because he hasn't invented it yet."

Houdini put down his fork and sat back in his chair. Then he began to laugh.

"Um, *excuse* me?" said Dash.

"*Ohh*, that's wonderful. He hasn't invented it yet . . ." Houdini put the side of his hand under his nose and laughed into it. "He doesn't even know the trick. That's just . . . that's marvellous." He hooted and wiped a tear that was trickling down his cheek.

"I tried to get him to come with us to Montreal—"

Houdini held his hand up. "I'm sorry," he said. "Forgive my mirth. It's been rather a dry month for laughter, I would say. But tell me, where is he, then?"

"He's still in Toronto."

Houdini leaned forward. "And he sent the two of *you* to negotiate with me?"

"We came on our own!" said Dash. "He didn't believe me either! So I made sure I got us here in order to find someone who maybe would!"

Houdini looked at the boy. His eyes glowing with warmth, he said, "Aren't you an enterprising young man, then."

"Yes, I am," said Dash, standing. "*I* got us here. To help Mr. Blumenthal get off his butt and invent his trick!"

"Whaddya mean *you* got us here!" Walt shouted. "It was *my* idea to get on the freight train!"

"Now, now, gentlemen." Houdini waited to be sure the outbursts were done. "You've both been through quite an ordeal. You may sit down, Master Woolf. You are attracting attention." When Dash had settled, Houdini said, "Look at you marvellous boys."

"Beg pardon?" said Walter.

"All alone, on an adventure. Maybe even telling the truth. You are rather brave."

"So you believe us?"

"Goodness, no. There's a difference between the truth and what people believe. I must tell you I am quite skeptical by nature. But I believe that *you* believe."

"What are you going to do when you see the newspaper tomorrow?" Dash asked.

At last Houdini signalled for the *escargots* to be taken away. Both boys sighed in relief. "I'll have those wrapped up for the beagles."

"You didn't answer my question," said Dash.

"After the morning paper comes," said Houdini, "I will send for you, and we will discuss your situation further." He considered them. "Are you sure you're not brothers?"

"Yessir, Mr. Houdini," said Walt. "I have a baby sister. That's it."

"And I'm an only child," said Dash.

"Who won't be born for another . . . seventy-four years." For some reason, Dash felt he had to look away. "Well, how lucky you are to have found each other, then."

"This is what the paper's gonna look like tomorrow morning," Dash said, stabbing the newspaper with his index finger. "That's Mr. Hopkins' picture. He's developing it right now, probably."

"And thus the future arrives," said Houdini, leaning toward them.

Afterwards, the bellman led them up the stairs beside the hotel desk and brought them to their room. Jacobson was waiting for them there, in the hallway outside number 508. The bellman opened the door and Dash and Walter walked through and stopped dead in their tracks.

It was an enormous room, with a wall-to-wall window overlooking downtown. White plumes rose from chimneys high into the cold, star-filled night.

"Oh my goodness," Walt whispered, moving farther into the room. "It's a palace!"

"I trust the room meets with your approval," said the bellman. Jacobson was putting a coin into his hand. "Thank you, sir," he said.

Jacobson looked around the room. "You're not to leave here until morning."

"Yes, sir," the boys replied.

"You will be woken at nine and given some breakfast. Harry will send for you when he is ready. Now, let us get on to other business." He turned smartly to Walt. "Master Gibson, your mother has given clear instructions on certain vitamins."

"Oh no," muttered Walt.

"She is concerned you may have insulted your constitution with such a long and unexpected train ride, and seeing as your sister is just recovering from a cold, she has instructed me to give you a proper dose of cod liver oil. Good thing given your sneezing, I'd say."

"This far, and she still reaches out to me with that cod liver oil."

"What is it?" asked Dash.

"Cod liver oil?" Jacobson removed a small, brown bottle from his suit jacket. "It is a miracle remedy for all manner of complaints. Ricketts, scoliosis, brittle hair and nails, anxious mothers . . ."

"It tastes like the inside of a shoe," said Walt. "I'd rather eat a plate of snails."

Jacobson looked amused. "Made from the steamed livers of codfish and then fermented in a barrel for a year. Served at room temperature from a spoon." He kissed his fingertips. "Delightful."

"I'm not having it," said Walt.

"Oh, you most certainly are," said Jacobson. "Your mother insists, and frankly, I wouldn't miss the opportunity."

He produced a spoon and unscrewed the cap of the bottle. Immediately, pungent waves of fishy-stink rose into the air. Jacobson poured a good dose of it into the spoon and held it out to Walt.

"You first," Walt said to him. "If you choke it down, I will."

Jacobson considered the spoon. Then, with a swift gesture, he plunged it into his mouth and swallowed. He gave no reaction at first, but then his right eyelid shuddered as if a small explosion had gone off in his brain. "Mmm," he said. "Yummy."

He refilled the spoon and held it out to Walt, who drank the oil with a look of unimpressed resignation. He was used to it.

"I'll have some," said Dash, and they both looked at him.

"Really?"

"Shouldn't I?"

"It *is* an occupational hazard of childhood," Jacobson said, refilling the spoon.

Dash put his head forward and drank the oil. It was warm and slippery. It had smelled pretty powerful, but going down, the taste wasn't all that bad. Then something that tasted old and sweaty and bitter rose into his throat. He put his hand over his mouth and ran into the washroom, gagging. It took six handfuls of water from the tap just to get rid of the urge to hurl. When he came out of the bathroom, Jacobson and Walt were doubled over laughing. There was a tear running down Jacobson's face.

"Oh, that *is* priceless," he said, snorting into his hand. "Well, if you need anything *else*, boys, use that bell there. And Harry's down the hall in 501."

"Okay!" said Dash, still waving his hand in front of his mouth. "Thank you very much, Mr. Jacobson."

"For the time being, you may call me Sol," he said. "But if you turn out *not* to be Harry's friends . . ." He didn't need to finish his sentence.

He put the key on one of the dressers and left.

"That was *horrible*," Dash said.

"Welcome to my world."

"You can keep it. Most of it. Not this room, though!" He looked around. "I'd like to keep being Houdini's guest for a night in 1926!"

"Me too!" said Walter. He ran and locked the door. Then he kicked off his shoes, jumped on the bed, and started bouncing. "Come on!" he called. "No one'll stop us!" He was jumping just high enough to get his hair to graze the ceiling.

Dash picked up a pillow and swung at Walter's ankles until he whacked him out of the air and Walter pinwheeled to the mattress. He lay there gasping with laughter.

"Oh yeah," he said, "you gotta try that."

Dash took his shoes off and jumped on the bed. Walter knocked him out of the air a few times with the pillow, and then they jumped around trying to navigate the room without touching the floor, moving from the mattress to a cushy chair to the couch, across the top of the dresser, and back to the bed. Finally they sat there, trying to catch their breath.

"Walter?" Dash said.

"What."

"You know this has already happened."

"Whaddya mean?"

"In my life, what's happening right now has already happened. And yet it *is* happening right now and it's never happened *before*. As far as I know."

Walt lay down and stared at the ceiling. "What if there are a lot of people out there from other times? Maybe you should find one of them and ask them what the heck to do!"

"It's possible, you know," Dash said. "That there would be others. Why would it only work for me?"

"I bet they're out there. People from the year four thousand and nine. Lookin' around. Hey, do you still have *Amazing Wonder Stories* in 2011?"

"What's that?"

"It's a *magazine*. Jeez. You don't have magazines?"

"We don't have *Amazing Wonder Stories*."

"Too bad. They had these spacemen time-travellers in one issue? They came in a rocket that was shaped like a butterfly."

"I didn't get here in a rocket ship. I was sent back against my will in a soap bubble."

"Right. Against your will, but for a reason." He turned over and looked up, lacing his fingers on his chest. "Maybe you're sapposta do something here."

"Yeah. Get home," Dash said, wanting the subject to be closed.

"Maybe it's something else."

Dash got off the bed and walked away. "Hey, where you going?" Walt said.

"Nowhere."

"Whaddid I say?"

Dash looked back at Walter. You could try not to think about something, but that didn't mean it wasn't there. Just like he'd been ignoring everything having to do with Alex leaving but still somehow thinking about it all the time. So it was with the nagging thought that he wasn't here just to get a magic trick invented.

"Remember I was telling you about the night of the vanish in 2011?" he asked.

"Yeah, what about it?"

"It was a special occasion. An anniversary." Walt sat at the edge of the bed now. "It was the eighty-fifth anniversary of Harry Houdini's death, is what it was."

There was an expectant look on Walt's face, like he was waiting to see where Dash was leading. And then he said, "Oh."

"On Halloween. Eleven days from now."

Walt looked down at the floor. "I wish you hadnta told me that."

"But I know how it happens," Dash said. "So maybe you're right. Maybe the reason we're here is to do something about it."

"You think we're here to save Harry Houdini?"

"No. Maybe. I don't know!"

"But can you do that?" Walt asked. "Is it even safe? What if you wreck *time*?"

"I saw a show once where a guy stepped on a bug in the past and everyone in the present turned into lizards. But maybe we can change *one little thing* without affecting anyone but Houdini. We wouldn't have to step on any bugs or anything."

"So what's the *one little thing*?"

"A punch in the stomach," said Dash, and then he explained.

17

Dash opened only one eye. The ceiling was made of panels of embossed tin. He looked to the left and saw a window looking out onto a city of buildings. White smoke came off the chimney pots atop a number of them. The sun was just rising.

He opened the other eye. He was still in the hotel room, and Walt was in the other bed, the covers pulled up over his shoulder. He was breathing softly. It was 1926. Although maybe he was in a coma somewhere. Maybe he was dead and this was some version of heaven.

He got out of the bed and used the washroom. He felt . . . *heavy* was the word. Like there was a weight on him. For the first time, he realized he felt sad. Not just scared and worried, but sad.

He'd already had his fill of this feeling when Alex left. It wasn't Alex's fault he had to go, but it still hadn't ended well. In the weeks leading up to their parting, the two boys had seen less and less of each other. Dash's mum had asked why, but all Dash could tell her was that Alex was acting like a jerk. He'd knock on the other boy's door and Alex's mother would say he wasn't feeling well and couldn't come out and play, but there was a look on her face that made Dash think she wasn't telling the truth. One of the last times they'd gone to the park, Alex had been a total pain, saying that Dash's slapshots were too hard, or that he hadn't scored when he had. He could *see* the little orange ball at the back of the net, but Alex kept saying it didn't count. Then he just announced that he had to go home, but it was still light out. Dash had enough money for two jawbreakers, but Alex had said he wasn't interested. He just scooped his ball up and walked out of the park.

After that, he wouldn't hang out. Dash hadn't seen him at all the last weeks Alex was in Toronto. Then, just before they left, Alex's mother had come by to drop off a letter from him. As Dash read the short letter, he listened to his mother talk to Alex's about how these kinds of things were hard for kids their age.

The letter just said, *Work on your slapshot. Have a nice life. Alex.*

"He didn't want to write anything," Alex's mother said to him. "But I didn't think it was proper. Do you want to send him anything back?"

"No," Dash had said. "It's okay. Tell him thanks."

She'd promised they would send an address once they were settled, but she hadn't yet. He wasn't sure why Alex had gotten so mad at him, but he was like that. People were like that. Nice one moment, mean the next. It had given him the heavy feeling he was having now, sitting on a toilet with a wooden seat in 1926, and it had taken weeks to go away.

It was almost nine in the morning. When he went back into the bedroom, Walt was still asleep. Dash went quietly to the door and opened it. There was a copy of the morning *Gazette* lying on the hallway carpet. He picked it up and sat on his bed with it.

The story was right where it was supposed to be. And the picture.

Someone had written at the edge of the paper: *There will be a car waiting for you downstairs at ten. Order breakfast. Put on your new clothes. I will see you at the Princess Theatre at 10:30. Harry.*

New clothes? He looked up and saw that there was a large white box on the nightstand. Someone had dropped it off in the night. It contained two days' change of undergarments and socks, two good pairs of pants, and two white shirts. There were also toothbrushes, tooth "powder," and a bar of soap.

"Walt," he said quietly. "Wake up."

Houdini had seen the paper. And now he wanted to see them.

You don't visit Harry Houdini in his dressing room wearing pants that have been soiled by snow, freight trains, pigs, and malt foam. The boys bathed and dressed and there was enough time to go down to the dining room and have croissants and orange juice. Honoré knew to put their breakfasts on Houdini's account.

They were on the sidewalk in front of the hotel at five to ten. A shiny black car—one *without* a canvas top—was parked down the street at the corner and as soon as they came out to the curb, the driver backed up to them. Dash opened the rear door and poked his head in.

"Is this Houdini's car?"

"You are Dashiel? And your friend is Walter?"

"Yes!" Dash gestured to Walter on the sidewalk and the two boys got in.

The driver smiled at them in the big rear-view mirror. He was wearing sunglasses and a cap. The boys sat and closed the door behind them and they were off.

For the first time in what felt like forever, Dash relaxed. He watched the city slide by through the back-seat window. He leaned forward and cranked the window down an inch so he could feel the cool air wash over him.

They'd come up with a simple plan. (For once.) While they were with Houdini, one of them would always be standing or sitting beside him, if possible. To reduce the opportunities Houdini's puncher would have. Dash knew Houdini's assailant had attacked him in the dressing room of the Princess Theatre . . . only he didn't know when. They'd have to be with him whenever he was in that room.

But if they stopped the punch . . .

The driver was speeding up now, driving away from downtown, Dash thought. "Sir? Where are we going?"

"Not far now," said the man.

Dash leaned against the door. "So you know what to do," he said to Walt.

"Yeah . . . I'll just watch and make sure no one makes any sudden moves."

On his left, through the window, Dash watched the mountain whip past. He was pretty sure the driver was getting lost. He leaned forward from the back seat. "Excuse me?" he asked. "Are you sure this is the way to the theatre?"

The driver turned in his seat. "What theatre, boys?"

He removed his sunglasses.

It was Frick!

Or Frack!

The worst kind of trick is one you don't see coming. This was Dash's thought when he saw the huge limestone building appear at the end of a curving driveway. It sat on a little hill all its own. A sign on the lawn said: CHILD WELFARE SERVICES—JUVENILE DETENTION.

"Oh no . . ." said Dash.

The driver said, "Mrs. Alphonsine is eager to welcome you."

"You have to take us back!" Dash protested. "We're meeting Houdini at the Princess Theatre."

"Sure you are," he said, grinning.

"Good grief!" muttered Walt. "Great move, Dash."

Frack or Frick put his sunglasses back on. It was turning out to be a beautiful, bright October morning, the kind where the smell of the fall leaves hangs in the air all day long. Dash wondered if they'd be able to smell the leaves from their cell. The driver parked at the top of the long curving driveway and led the boys into the building.

Inside, they were left in a cold antechamber filled with stone columns. The big wooden doors closed behind him.

"Don't worry," said Dash. "Houdini will figure out what happened."

Walt leaned against a pole, glowering. "We're doomed now."

Mrs. Alphonsine appeared out of the stony gloaming. "How nice to see you poor boys again. Come in and get into your uniforms. We're about to have lunch. You'll meet everyone properly then."

"No way!" said Walt, slapping at her hand. "I wanna call my dad!"

"Now, now, don't make me call the Andrés."

"Who are the Andrés?" Walter growled.

"You met them at that disgusting palace of gluttony we *almost* rescued you from last night. Now, at least, you are safe."

"Can we come back later?" Dash asked hopefully. "This seems like a really nice place. I had it all wrong."

"Yeah, we'll come back later," Walt said, sauntering to the door. It opened just as he got there and their driver stepped in.

"Ah, André, here you are. Maybe you will show these boys to the dormitory where they can get changed for lunch."

"*Oui, madame.*" He snatched Dash up under one arm, Walt under the other.

"You have to let us go!" shouted Dash. "We have to save Harry Houdini!"

"Mr. Houdini is a grown man. He will have to decide whether he wants to be saved or not. As for you boys, cooperate or André will have to settle you down."

They settled down enough to get their feet under them and walk.

"That's better," said Mrs. Alphonsine.

The boys of the detention centre filed into the cavernous mess hall. Dash and Walt, in their grey cloth uniforms, walked side by side to the table one of the orderlies pointed them to. There was a piano at the front of the room, where a nun sat waiting. Mrs. Alphonsine stepped toward the piano and nodded to her.

"Let us sing grace," she said, and the pianist in her dainty wimple began to play. All but two young men in the hall raised their voices in a high, bright note that filled the room and seemed to go on and on.

Lunch was much worse than anything they'd actually been fearing. *Escargots* were fine dining, compared to this. Everything was more or less the same colour. It was so dreadful that it will not be spoken of.

Walt's mood had declined further by the time they were brought back to the dorm after lunch. He harangued Dash, telling him that if *he'd* been in charge, he would have found them a nice jalopy to ride in from Toronto to Montreal and there would have been *no* pigs and *no* angry rail bull with an apple-shaped bruise on his forehead, and there would certainly be *no* Mrs. Alphonsina or whatever her name was, serving them gruel on dented tin plates!

"And maybe, right now, we'd be stopping someone from punching your precious Houdini!"

Their fellow inmates tried as best they could not to notice them. Some glanced their way once or twice, heads down, as if shyly, but Dash knew they were afraid. He'd read some of Charles Dickens in school. He knew what happened to kids in orphanages and foster homes who got out of hand. They caught the side of a cane. And apparently, it really hurt. Maybe as much as a rail bull's truncheon.

"Keep your voice down, okay, Walt? We don't need to get into any more trouble."

"Just let 'em try to shut me up! I'm a citizen, you know! I'll give 'em holy heck!"

At the word *holy*, many heads jerked down between shoulder blades. Dash put his hand on Walt's arm and Walt looked at it like he was going to eat it. Dash removed his hand.

"Maybe history doesn't want to be changed," Dash said.

"So what."

"So maybe this was always going to happen."

"SO WHAT."

"So it's not my fault."

In the afternoon, it was calisthenics. Walt glared at him the entire time they did stride jumps in the yard. The *entire* time, his head sideways, staring at Dash with wrath. He was a hothead, thought Dash, counting to a hundred. It was catechism in the afternoon (Walt: eyes wide open, staring ahead, arms tensed, ready to kill), and then more gruel in the evening (Walt:

dripping glops of horror back onto his plate, not eating, silent). Bedtime was *seven o'clock!*

They'd missed the whole day. For all Dash knew, maybe they'd already missed their chance, and Houdini was getting ready for his evening show with a deep, spreading pain in his belly. From—he would be thinking—a punch.

They were given hard toothbrushes to clean their teeth with. They lined up with the other boys to use one of the three sinks in the bathroom. The line was silent as the boys shuffled forward. As they got closer, Dash heard Walt behind him, laughing.

"Hey," he was saying to someone, "what are you in for?"

Dash turned around. Walt was talking to the kid behind him. The kid's face was a terrified blank.

"Steal a horse?" asked Walt. "What about you?"

The kid standing behind the kid with the stone face put his fingers to his lips.

"Me 'n' Dashiel here—he's from the future, so he's already broken a whole bunch of laws, like lawsa *nature*—but I attacked a policeman. Got us in a stir, boys! But don't worry. Dash's got a plan—right, Dash?"

"Uh-huh," said Dash, quietly.

"He's got a space car from TWO THOUSAND an' eleven. Gonna zap it here, pick us up, take us out for steaks during the Roman Empire, then we're gonna visit Golgotha for hot milk before we go to bed on the moon in umpty-million and four."

There was stomping in the hall. One of the Andrés swung

down the line, his big hands clenching and unclenching at his sides. "*Who* is speaking?" he rasped in a murderous voice.

"OH!" said Walt. "You're just in time, sir. My friend and I would like to have our car brought round. We're not going to stay at Hotel Slop-de-Poop any longer."

The man's hand darted out and grabbed Walt by the ear. "You will come with me now," he said, pulling him out of the line.

Walt grimaced in pain. "This is no way to treat a guest," he said, and the man tugged harder.

"Sir!" cried Dash. "He doesn't mean—" but he didn't get the rest of the sentence out before he felt the man's other hand clamp down on *his* ear.

"Misery loves company." André pulled them both away.

Not a soul in the line looked up as they went past, nor did anyone speak a word.

The man yanked them down the long, cold hall. They had to stay bent over and keep up a good pace to ensure their ears stayed attached to their heads. He said nothing to them until they arrived at a set of stairs, which he all but pitched them down. "Go," he said.

They went. Three flights to a darkened hallway. It got colder.

They heard stirring in the darkness.

He pushed them along and they felt the wall to their right. Dash's hand slipped into an opening.

"In there," said one of the Andrés, and they went into a small room with no light at all and heard a door close.

Then footsteps receding.

Then silence.

"Happy now?" said Dash into the darkness.

"Delighted. I noticed your pal Houdini didn't try to get us out."

"I'm sure he and Sol are looking for us. We disappeared."

"Ha." Walt gave a humourless wheeze. "Maybe they think we skipped back to 1809."

"Someone will come." Dash looked over at his frightened friend. "Nothing's going to happen to us, Walt. But you know what this means, don't you? Houdini has no one to protect him!"

18

The night passed in agonizing slowness. In the near-dark—a candle lit the hallway to the cells—Walt's silence was terrible to Dash. He knew how frightened Walt was now, because anyone would have been frightened. Dee Dee's cold seemed to be really getting to him as well. He sniffled and shivered in the corner. Dash felt fear crawl up and down his back and then to his stomach, like an eel was winding its way around his insides. All night long, they'd fall asleep only to come awake with sudden awareness and glance around, scared to move their heads.

One of the times Dash awoke he found Walt asleep with his eyes open. He was staring into space, and his mouth was agape. His breathing was raspy. Walt's face looked dead and it filled Dash with a feeling so powerful he thought he might be sick. He looked away and tried to close his eyes again, but he felt Walt staring at some space beyond the bars that Dash, too, could see.

How convincing was Walt's dream? he wondered. Some people knew they were dreaming, but Dash wasn't one of them.

Dash heard a soft scuffling in the hallway. The entrance to the cell was the size of a large cupboard door, but from where he was sitting, Dash could see out into the hallway that led to the stairs. Someone was coming down. More than one person.

"Come on, then," said a British-accented voice.

More candles were lit on the way, and the hallway opened with light. It was larger than Dash had thought. In fact, it was a room. There was a bar along one of the walls, and as a man came forward lighting candles, people flowed in behind him. Men and women, many of them dressed in jeans! And T-shirts!

A neon light flickered to life against the wall behind the bar. It said HARRY'S.

People were talking and laughing. They began to seat themselves and hold up their hands for waiters and barmen. It was full of life in there.

A man with a black beard came to the cell door. "Get out of there!" he said.

Dash pushed open the door. It hadn't been locked. He stepped out.

As soon as he did, a woman jumped up and rushed to him from one of the tables, where she'd been eating nachos with her friends. "Harry!" she cried out, coming to him with widespread arms. Nachos? "Thank God you're here. We were worried about you! Worried to *death*!" She gathered him up in her arms.

"I'm not Harry," he said.

"What?" she said angrily. "Then what are you doing here?"

And his eyes flew open and the candle was out. He heard Walt's wet breathing in the darkness. The world was completely empty.

Dash had no idea what time it was. It seemed hours had passed since they'd been brought what was called "breakfast." It had to be at least noon.

It had begun to feel that maybe they would be stuck here until Walt's parents came and got them—as they eventually, inevitably would—but how long would that take? It was hard to imagine that both Jacobson and Houdini would have abandoned them.

Surely the punch had already occurred and the two men had bigger problems to deal with. Dash felt his spirits ebb. Walter wouldn't talk to him at all, and anyway, what was there to talk about? Nothing had worked out as planned. And if Houdini got out of Montreal without so much as *considering* if he would help Blumenthal, then Dash was going to be stuck in 1926. And Houdini was going to die, as he always had, on Halloween.

"Lunch," said Walter listlessly. "Lucky us."

There were footsteps coming down the stairs. "I'm not hungry either," Dash said.

But it was Mrs. Alphonsine. "I know two very lucky boys," she said. "Your father has come to get you," she said. Walt jumped up. "What are you doing?" she said to Dash.

"I guess I'm sitting here."

"You think he's only taking Master Gibson here? I should think not. Get up. He's agreed to take you both."

Thank god, thought Dash, and he felt weary with relief.

"I'm in a bucketa water now," Walt said. He looked pale in the light.

Mrs. Alphonsine stood on the other side of the cramped, open doorway and leaned down to beckon them out.

She herded them up the stairs and into the high, stone antechamber at the front of the foster home. Then down another hallway, this one panelled in a deep red wood, to an office with her name on the door. She pushed the door open and let them in.

"My boys! My poor boys!" cried Herman Blumenthal, opening his arms wide.

Six miles away, in the heart of the city, in the dressing room of the Princess Theatre, Harry Houdini was sitting for a drawing. The artist, a student named Sam Smilovitz, was drawing him in pencil as he lay back on the divan, reading his mail and chatting with his guests, who included another student, Jack Price, and a man named Gordon Whitehead. Whitehead was pontificating on a method he claimed to have invented for vanishing birds. Houdini listened patiently.

His mail had arrived at the hotel desk that morning. Requests for autographs, catalogues, bills for equipment and repairs, bills for advertising. He wasn't really listening to Whitehead. There was always a blowhard nearby regaling him with tales of his own feats. Had Mr. Whitehead dangled upside down from a chain over the streets of Chicago while in a straitjacket? And escaped from it? He had a feeling Mr. Whitehead might need a straitjacket, but the venue for his performance wouldn't be outdoors in front of a crowd of thousands.

But now something he said caught Houdini's attention. Whitehead was standing behind the divan talking about his own strength. How he could bend an inch-wide iron bar between his two hands. Jack Price was sitting beside the man he called "Smiley" and looking at the developing sketch.

Whitehead was going on. "Is it true, Harry, that you can withstand a blow to your abdomen without sustaining any injury at all?"

"Well," said Houdini, but he stopped speaking when he saw Jack Price's face go white.

Whitehead came forward in what seemed to be slow motion, but before Houdini could even begin to imagine what was going on, the man had dealt him a hard blow. It struck him with great force directly below his ribs, driving him back down into the cushions and knocking the air out of him. A wave of pain bloomed behind his eyes and flooded his body. But Whitehead did not stop. He punched Houdini again on the right side and then the left side of his belly, both terrible clouts that were audible to everyone in the room. The students were immediately on their feet, clutching at Whitehead, pulling him away.

"That will do," said Houdini, standing. He gestured to Smiley and Jack Price to release Gordon Whitehead. His belly felt bruised, but he stood tall and showed no sign of the pain he felt. This was his public, like them or not. "That was an excellent attempt, Gordon, and I admire your vanish technique. I will have to keep my wits about me as the younger generation learns their craft."

"I am impressed myself," said Whitehead. "You can really take a punch." He offered to shake hands, and Houdini did.

19

Mrs. Alphonsine delivered a brief lecture on the natural evils of young boys, and how responsible fathers keep track of them. Then she said someone would return with their things and she went out in a cloud of righteousness.

Then Walt punched Herman Blumenthal in the stomach.

"OOF," grunted Blumenthal, taking a couple of steps backwards.

"*Now* you come?" said Walt.

"I wasn't ready for that," said the magician, holding his gut.

"Don't hit him again!" Dash rushed over to Blumenthal and took him by the forearm. "How did you find us?"

"I got in last night," he said. "Found Houdini's hotel this morning. A waiter told me you were goin' down to the theatre . . . so I went. You weren't there."

"No kidding," said Walt.

"Was Houdini there?" asked Dash.

"I didn't see him." Blumenthal stood up straight, breathing

again. "I guess I deserved that," he said to Walt. "Truce, though! No punching a guy in the stomach when he's not expectin' it. An uncle a' mine took a haymaker in the liver and he passed away!"

Dash and Walt exchanged a look.

"Okay, truce," said Dash.

Walt looked like he was going to be hard about it, but then he muttered, "Fine," and said, "I'm not mad anymore. I just wanna get out of here. And I was expecting my dad!"

"You'll see your dad soon enough," Blumenthal reassured him.

"You didn't say how you found us," Dash said.

"I met Houdini's manager. He was out of his mind with worry."

"How come *he* didn't come looking for us then?"

"He knew you were here. But they wouldn't release you to him. Only to a parent."

Walt guffawed. "And they believed *you* were *my* dad?"

"No," said Blumenthal. "But they believed I was his." He looked at Dash.

Dash looked away. It was a little embarrassing.

"You coulda' believed me sooner!" Dash said.

"Who says I believe you? I figured out how to do the trick. I'm gonna sell it to Houdini."

"What?"

"He came all this way for fifty bucks, Dash."

"Don't sell him the trick." Dash said. "Promise me."

"You like me poor? You liked me at the Century, huh? You think that's where I belong?"

"Look, Mr. Blumenthal—this is your trick. You have to perform it!"

"He's just in it for the money!" shouted Walter.

"Shut up!" Dash rounded on him. "I'm tryna talk to Mr. Blumenthal. Please," he said, imploring the man. "Just ask for his help. I bet he'll give it. This is your trick."

"What if I sell it to him, but I reserve the right to premiere it? That doesn't change anything for you."

Walter had started laughing. "This is the guy who's gonna save you, eh?"

Dash ignored him. He kept his eyes clamped on Blumenthal's. "Don't sell him the trick," he said. If you do, it might never get performed. And I'll be stuck here forever.

"What's wrong with here, kid?"

"AND—you'll never be famous and no one will want you and you'll never have a magic family—"

"OK!" said Blumenthal. "I won't sell him the trick!" He looked at the two boys. "What? You wanna stay here a bit longer? Let's go!"

Sol Jacobson was standing in front of the magician's door at the Prince of Wales like a guard. When they approached, he looked both relieved and annoyed. "I thought you were putting them on a train," he said to Blumenthal.

"I didn't say when." He chucked his chin at the door to room 501. "Is Mr. Houdini home?"

"He's resting."

"When will he *not* be resting, then?"

"I am unable to provide that information, Mr. Blumenthal."

Herman Blumenthal closed one eye. "Everything okay, Mr. Jacobson?"

"Can we please go in?" said Dash. "Please? There's a threat against Houdini's life!"

"Yes, we *met* the threat," said Jacobson, advancing and lowering his voice. "Its name was Whitehead. I don't suppose any of you three know the fisticuffal Mr. Whitehead, do you?"

"No," said Blumenthal. "Who is Mr. Whitehead?"

So it had already happened. "He punched Houdini," said Dash glumly.

"*Exactly*," said Sol Jacobson. "And how would *you* know that?"

"How would I know it?" Dash shouted, and Jacobson started and stepped backwards. "How would I know it? Because I'm from the future, you stubborn old donkey!" His fists were clenched at his sides. "Well, is he okay at least?"

Small droplets of sweat had formed on Jacobson's upper lip. "Yes," he said quietly. "He's all right."

The door opened. Houdini was standing in it with a black housecoat cinched around his waist. "Sol," he said. "What is all the shouting about— Oh, hello, boys! You made it out! What a bother! You must come in and fortify yourselves. Come on, Sol, let them in."

Sol stood aside looking disenchanted, and Houdini brought them in and made them sit on the divan.

"You, I don't know," Houdini said to Blumenthal, and the other magician extended his hand with a kind of shyness that Dash was surprised to see.

"Herman Blumenthal, Mr. Houdini."

"Harry," whispered Walt. "Just call him Harry."

"Ah, *the* Blumenthal! Well, come in."

"If you need your rest—"

"Nonsense. Sol, let's get these boys something hot and something sweet, and Mr. Blumenthal something in the way of beefsteak and . . .?"

"A glassa tomato juice."

Sol went to the telephone to order up some supplies. He was not a happy man. Dash had seen a flash of fear in his eye.

Houdini settled into a chair.

"Are you okay?" Dash asked him.

"Am *I* okay? You two went missing!"

"We got in the wrong car. But you were *attacked*!"

"Oh, old fusspot told you, did he?" He looked over at Sol and rolled his eyes at him. "I'm fine."

"You're not fine," said Jacobson. "Now you have a broken ankle *and* a gut-ache. I always tell you, Harry, not everyone is a well-wisher!"

Houdini dismissed his friend's comments with a wave of his hand. "I've been punched before and I'll be punched again. What do you think, boys?" He patted his belly with both hands. "Would you like to take a shot?"

Dash and Walt shook their heads emphatically no.

"So," he said. "It would seem this morning's *Gazette* bears up your story."

"Flimflam!" said Jacobson. He stood with his back to them, flipping paper at a table. "Or witchcraft."

"It's 1926, Solomon. We don't believe in witchcraft anymore."

He turned in anger to Houdini. "If you believe them, you're more gullible than the old ladies handing their money over to the mediums!"

"Why don't you go wet your whistle, Sol?"

"My whistle is fully moistened, Harry. But I'll go check on the food."

After he left, Houdini sighed. "It is hard to be close to anyone," he said. "People do have their limits."

"Mr. . . . Harry," said Blumenthal. "This boy must have told you about the vanish he claims he was in."

"*Was* in," said Dash matter-of-factly.

"I believe I know how to do it."

"Well, then, you must be a very good magician," said Houdini, "but I know how to do it as well. Up to a point." He looked at Dash with a slightly comic expression on his face.

Blumenthal fiddled with his hat in his lap. "He says it must be *my* trick."

"Well, go on, then. Take it. I have plenty of tricks." He turned to the boys. "And I hope you will come and see some of them."

"He needs your help," said Dash. "I think we're all supposed to help *each other*."

"I see," said Houdini. "And how is it that you help *me*?"

"I . . ." Dash began, but Blumenthal interrupted him.

"I am prepared to sell you a share in it, if you like."

Dash glared at him.

"Why would I buy a trick I already know how to do?"

"Because if, on the off-chance, it works as young Master Woolf here says it does, it may be something you would be pleased to have a share in. And perhaps it only works the way he says it does if *I* am the one who performs the trick."

"He *is* the one who performs the trick," said Dash. "It's *his* trick, you can't buy it."

Houdini looked perplexed for a moment. "You don't *want* me to help him now?"

"I do. But it's *his* trick. He does it, and . . . and you come and watch it."

"What?" This from both Blumenthal and Walt.

"Yeah. He comes and watches."

"Why?"

Dash looked at the immortal, all-too-mortal magician. "So he sees it for himself."

Blumenthal shrugged. "Sure, why not? He can come. Why don't we split the proceeds?" he said to Houdini.

But something in the turn of the conversation had made Harry Houdini uncomfortable. He looked around the room. "What are you three plotting?"

"Nothing," said Dash. "But you should see it. Because if it works—"

There was a knock at the door. Houdini rose, then thought better of it and sat down again. Dash had seen him wince.

"You're in pain."

"I have a gastritis," Houdini said, waving off his concern. "I get it frequently. Hotel food, restaurant food—"

"A punch in the gut," said Walt.

Houdini sat up straight, his face set, and there was no evidence that he was in any discomfort at all now, even as he leaned toward his guests. A man came in with a large black tray laden with plates of delicious-smelling food.

"I know pain, gentlemen. Pain is my constant companion. I would be dead if it were not for pain and physical suffering. Could I do what I do if I feared it? If it were not in fact my friend? The show goes on. The show is everything."

"But don't you think you should see a doctor?"

Houdini stood. He unbuttoned his shirt and removed it. The man putting out the steak and the bowls of stew stood back. There was a small, red welt still glowing on the left side of Houdini's torso. His stomach was tapered and muscular—it looked corrugated. Houdini held his left arm out to his side and he made a fist. The sinews in his arms popped out. He brought his fist down suddenly, in an arc toward his own body. It landed with a sharp slap in the centre of the welt. Harry Houdini's face didn't change. He did it again, hard.

"Don't," said Dash. "Stop."

"This is not pain, young man."

"Fine. Stop it."

"No punch can fell Erich Weiss! Erich Weiss crushes stones in his hands!" He put his shirt back on and sat down. He gave the stunned waiter a couple of coins and then gestured to the food to invite them to eat. "That is *boeuf bourguignon*," he said, waving his fingers at the bowls of stew. "If you don't like *that*, there's no hope for you."

They liked it just fine. And when every bit of china had been practically licked clean, and every piece of cutlery as well, Houdini said, "All right. I'll help you, Herman Blumenthal. I'll have the trick built and take half the proceeds it generates. However it works." He turned his eye on each of them, an eyebrow cocked. "But only because I can't resist a good story."

20

Jacques Pelletier was a theatrical builder with a workshop in a huge, hangar-like building in Old Montreal near the water, on a street called Rue du Port. He supplied many of the theatres in Montreal with their sets, props, and even costumes for all kinds of shows, big and small. He employed a dozen people—welders, sewers, carpenters, painters, sculptors, riggers—to make it all. He was happy to welcome Houdini and his entourage in the afternoon. The two magicians and Pelletier hunched over Blumenthal's sketches while Jacobson and Walt looked around the workshop.

Dash's mood had changed: nothing he said or did seemed to have the power to get Houdini to take his injury more seriously. And Blumenthal had managed to do business, despite Dash's objections. He'd gotten Houdini excited about the trick—they'd pored over the drawings after lunch—and when Jacobson had returned, they'd explained their plan to him.

Jacobson was as nonplussed as Dash, but for a different reason: he was furious that Houdini was being hospitable to a trio of strangers he'd sooner see on a train *out* of Montreal. And when he heard that Houdini had agreed to see the trick in Toronto, he'd flown into a rage. Finally, he struck a bargain: if Harry insisted, he could have the trick built, but he *wasn't* getting off the train in Toronto. Enough was enough! He groaned when he heard that Houdini was going to give half the proceeds to Blumenthal, but at least he'd won on the other front. And anyway, what was Harry going to do? Cancel his show in Detroit Saturday night?

That was exactly what Dashiel Woolf had been thinking. If he had failed to stop the punch, he could still prevent Houdini from meeting his fate in Detroit by getting him to stop in Toronto. But Jacobson had squashed even that hope. He waited by the door of the warehouse, despondent. He'd arrived in Montreal just wanting to get home, but the growing belief that he was supposed to help Houdini was casting a shadow over every thought. It felt like the cosmos was going to get in his way in whatever way it could.

It was cold inside the building, which had steel walls and a high, curved ceiling, but there were stoves scattered here and there throughout, and a small cadre of men and women hustled around the place carrying bits of scenery. Originally—Pelletier had explained—the building had been used as a cold-storage facility for meat and fish (there were docks on the river not fifty feet away) but it had fallen into disuse, and twenty years ago he'd converted it.

Dash looked out the door at the cobblestone streets. This old part of the city made him feel like he'd time-travelled *again*.

Maybe if he stuck around long enough he'd meet some Indians in birchbark canoes.

He felt a hand come down on his shoulder. It was Jacobson. "I don't know what you boys are really up to," he said.

"We're not up to anything," Dash replied sullenly. "Harry offered to help Blumenthal and I guess I'm just along for the ride now."

"Like fun you are." Jacobson held out a small paper wallet. "These are two tickets back to Toronto for you and your little partner in crime," he said. "You leave at 10 a.m."

"I'm not leaving until Blumenthal has the trick. Would you?"

"I'm *doing* what I would do. I'm sending you two jacka-napeses back to where you came from. Your parents should be dealing with you, not us. Take these."

Dash took the wallet. There were two printed train tickets inside. Jacobson was regarding him with something in his eyes that looked strangely like fear.

"You believe us," Dash said.

"I don't know what I believe. All I know is that I've heard enough." He pushed past Dash into the street beyond the work-shop and put on his hat. "So be it."

"Where are you going?"

"I have a letter to write," he said.

"And you trust us . . . *jackanapeses* . . . with your poor, help-less friend?"

"Harry will have to take care of himself."

He turned a corner and was gone.

Dash had the instinct to follow him. What use would he be here now, with Houdini already injured, already sick? He closed the door to Pelletier's workshop and went out into the cool afternoon air. But when he turned the corner where Jacobson had gone, the man was nowhere in sight.

Maybe the big lesson in all of this was that life could be as crummy in the past as it was in the present. He'd begun to notice that bad things hurt him more than good things made him feel good. Alex's absence in his life was not getting easier as time went on. And he didn't have anyone to take his place. Obviously, Walt wasn't going to be a new, lifelong pal. Walter would be ninety-six in 2011. That was a stretch for anyone. Dash didn't think he'd even ever met a person who was ninety-six. What a depressing thought.

He walked into the thin, quiet streets of Old Montreal. It was tomblike; for a while he saw no other people at all. The buildings were old and made of square, smooth stone that seemed to catch the air and send it back even colder.

He arrived on another street and there were some people here. There was a small grocery store and a restaurant selling crepes through a window. It was very cold out, but he walked at a good pace and stayed warm. It felt, in the silence and stillness, like there were eyes on him. He looked up from time to time into the big bright windows in the old buildings, but they were all empty. The hair on the back of his neck stood up.

He went out of the Old City and back into downtown, keeping his eyes peeled for stray pigs. He avoided the train station.

Although, for a moment he considered going in and just jumping a train back to Toronto. Who would notice anyway? He didn't belong to anyone here, and in 2011 he'd already vanished, so it wouldn't be a stretch just to disappear completely. The world would go on without him. It was going to do that anyway. Even if Blumenthal got the trick built, it wasn't going to make him famous. It *hadn't* made him famous in the world Dash lived in. And if time was time, forever and unchangeable, then Herman would *never* be famous. Never rich. Never great.

He heard a voice calling to him as he approached Rue Sainte-Catherine. A fearful thrill went through him. He *knew* someone had been following him. He turned around and saw a policeman ambling up. Was there a reward on his head?

"Good afternoon, young man," he said. He was a large, round officer with a ring of keys on his hip. His badge said *Constable Montrose.* "You enjoying our chilly autumn weather?"

"Oh, it's *fine* weather," said Dash. "Yes, sir! Thank you!"

"Where are your parents, boy?"

"My mum is finishing her tea in the hotel," said Dash calmly. "She gave me permission to buy sweets."

"Well, don't go now and rot your teeth."

"I won't, sir. Honest. I'll floss and everything."

"You'll do what now, son?"

"Floss?"

A small clatch of people was gathering. Dash began to feel nervous.

"And what hotel are your parents in?"

"Prince of Wales."

"Uh-huh," said the policeman. He was removing a little black book from his pocket. "And what would your name be?"

"I'm, uh, Marty McFly and . . . um, and—"

"I see." He was writing. He paused to look over the top of his notebook. "Where on earth did you get those shoes, son?"

"Oh, I, uh, my mother is an experimental shoemaker, and she, she—" He could feel the energy building up in his legs.

"She what?" said Montrose.

"She's always coming up with ideas," said a man in the crowd. He stepped forward.

"Dad?" Dash said.

But it wasn't his father. It was a man who walked like him, and who, when he smiled at Dash, smiled just like his father.

"Come on, buddy. Your mother and I are waiting for you at the hotel." He offered his hand.

In his peripheral vision, Dash saw Constable Montrose put his notebook away. Dash looked in the man's eyes and saw his kind expression.

"We don't want to keep her waiting, now, do we, Dash?"

He felt like he was going to faint. "Yeah . . . don't want to keep her waiting."

"Nothing to see! Move along!" sang Montrose, and he tipped his cap to the man. Dash noticed he wore a black, featureless ring on his lapel.

When they were alone, Dash, his voice full of awe, said, "Who are you?"

"You'll understand who I am later. Just get back down there. You want to spend every minute you can with him, don't you?"

"Houdini?"

"No, buddy. Not Houdini. Now go."

Dash walked south in a stupor, toward the boundary of the Old City with its mazelike streets, and then he vanished into them like a deer into a forest. When he arrived back at Pelletier's workshop, he was breathing hard. He clutched his shirt and forced himself to breathe normally.

When he'd calmed down a little, he stood up and looked through the window in the workshop door. There was no one there.

There was also no one in the old warehouse. There had been half a dozen people here before.

"Not again," Dash muttered.

He walked in cautiously, shaking out his hands, which had begun tingling when the man appeared. He was still breathing hard. "Hello?" he called.

Then he heard sounds from the back of the workshop. There were voices, the faint dinging of metal objects. He followed the sounds and came to the edge of a space he hadn't seen before: a miniature stage, complete with lights, in the corner of the warehouse. And Houdini was standing on it, with everyone from the workshop around him. There were a few chairs in rows on risers. At the edge of the small crowd, Blumenthal and Walt stood watching.

Dash remained in the shadows.

"Bring up the lights again, Jacques," said Houdini from the stage. The warehouse lights came back on. "Oh yes, I can still see the upper ring should be quite a bit smaller. We want one to fit just inside the other. Or perhaps— Jacques?"

"*Oui, maître?*"

"Do you think there could be a bevel in the upper ring? What if the edge interferes when it comes back up? No, hold on. That makes it less stable on the bottom. I think it should be smaller."

"*Charlot? Tu là?*" called Pelletier from the light board. A man at the side of the stage answered. "*Peux tu couper la boucle?*" Pelletier asked him.

"*Oui, chef!*"

"*Vas-y, donc.*"

Houdini passed the ring to the man who stepped forward. "I don't know," he said. "Something is wrong. Why doesn't everyone go back to what they were doing. I'm sure Monsieur Pelletier has got you doing important work for your other clients."

Most of them dispersed, although a couple couldn't help stepping forward to shake the great man's hand.

When they had all gone back to their stations, Houdini stepped toward Walt and Blumenthal. Dash watched them talking, but he couldn't hear what they were saying. Houdini made shapes with his hands; Blumenthal nodded.

Walter saw him standing in the shadows and gestured: *where have you been?* Dash remained where he was. Finally the other boy came out of the light and walked up to him.

"What's going on? Where'd you go?"

"I went for a walk."

"You leaving us here to solve your problems for you?"

"Oh, excellent!" said Harry Houdini, "you're just in time." He wasn't talking to Dash, though. Jacobson had returned. He was holding an envelope in his hands. "Come look at this, see if you can't figure out the problem with the sheath we've put in."

"I don't wish to look." Jacobson came forward slowly. "In fact, I've come to tender my resignation."

"Solomon." Houdini held his arms out to him. "Solomon. Why don't we skip the resigning and second thoughts and just make up now. You are quite right, I get carried away with myself. My dangerous enthusiasms, isn't that how you put it?"

"I am finished, Harry. You won't listen to anybody. I hire bodyguards, you won't use them. Bess herself asks you to cancel a show so you can take two days off for a broken ankle, but here you are in Montreal, charming them in two tongues. Well, you won't charm me anymore. If I were just your manager, I would be happy to count the receipts, but I am your friend and I won't be a part of this."

"Come now," said Houdini, trying to draw him back into the lit part of the room. "Everyone has moments of doubt. But you must push *through*, not turn back. What would have happened if I had ever turned back, Sol?"

"You'd be a rabbi."

Houdini laughed. "Perhaps. But I would never have been Houdini."

"Erich Weiss was good enough for me, Harry. I'm sorry."

Dash saw the man was decided. No amount of talking was going to change his mind. Houdini saw it as well.

"Well," he said. "What a sad tune I am hearing. And at a moment when something genuinely miraculous might be before us."

"What? From these devils? Sent from where, to pour what treacle in your ear?"

"Hey!" said Walt, rushing toward him. "At least we don't abandon each other!" He came to a stop just below Jacobson's nose. "Go, then! We can take care of ourselves!"

"Don't miss your train, Master Gibson," Jacobson said. "Or perhaps you may find yourself back in the care of the municipality."

Walt pushed his face up into Jacobson's and growled at him, "And I wonder how *that* would happen?"

"I'm a manager," he said, smiling meanly. "I manage things."

Walt's hand shot out and he shoved Jacobson backwards forcefully. There was a full two-foot difference in height between them, but Walt was strong. Jacobson stumbled away and Walt came after him, pulling a fist back behind his ear, but Jacobson caught it as it came whizzing forward and he hauled Walt down into a headlock. Suddenly it was pandemonium: their two bodies were writhing on the floor amidst shouts and imprecations. Dash ran to them and grabbed Walt, as Houdini, Herman Blumenthal, and Pelletier attempted to pry Jacobson off the boy.

"Gerroff!" cried Walt, while at the same time trying to rip

tufts of hair out of Jacobson's head. "Gettim off me!"

"I'll show you what I do to cheats and charlatans!" the other man bellowed.

People ran up from parts of the workshop. Houdini had almost interposed himself between the two of them and he was pushing Jacobson away with his back while holding Walt at arm's length.

"Stop it!" he said. "Stop it immediately."

At last the two were separated.

"I'm gonna . . . I'll tear out . . . the resta . . ." said Walt, gasping for air. "Ya big bully!"

"Keep that child away from me. Keep them both away from me!"

"Ya better keep looking over yer shoulder!" rasped Walt. His face was pale and shining and his eyes were wild. "Ya better . . ." he said, but then he leaned forward into Houdini and closed his eyes. "I'm gonna," he said quietly, and then he slipped down the front of Houdini's suit and fell to the floor in a heap.

"Now look what you've done," said Jacobson.

21

Walter was out cold. To Dash, he looked like a gleaming white sculpture against the black floor. Jacobson and Houdini were staring daggers at each other.

"We'd best get the business of your scarpering off taken care of, then," Houdini said, "so those of us left behind can get this poor boy to a doctor."

"Don't do me a melodrama, Harry. It's not my fault you've never seen a dodge like this."

Blumenthal gave Dash a look that was supposed to calm him down, except it didn't.

What was wrong with Walt? He hadn't even hit his head, but his eyes were closed.

"It's not a dodge," said Houdini. "Or if it is, it deserves the attention of the greatest magician alive. Is that not what you would say, Solomon? Even if this young man—oh, someone get that boy a glass of water, stop standing around!—has not come from the future with strange news . . ." He looked at Dash now.

Four glasses of water arrived at once from different directions. Someone had the presence of mind to bring a wet cloth. "Even if . . ."

Jacobson looked at Dash with cold mistrust in his eyes. His mouth moved, but for a moment he said nothing. Then: "I will keep my letter and see to Walter first. I'll bring him back to your room and have the doctor you won't listen to take a look at him. I will telegram his parents to inform them of the situation, and then I will put him on the 10 a.m. train tomorrow morning. And now I will take his ticket, Master Woolf."

Houdini watched the ticket change hands. "He'd already given you those?" he said to Dash.

"He made me take them—I wasn't going to leave. I'm staying." He kept his gaze on the floor, unable to look up. "But I guess . . . Walt should go home."

Jacobson put the ticket into a suit pocket. "When this is done, my resignation will take effect. I will update the letter."

"Maybe I will accept it," said Houdini. "If that is the best thing to do."

"Dmitri!" Jacobson called. A man appeared instantly. He was dressed in a uniform and a cap. Houdini's driver. A small, muscular man with bright, grey eyes behind thick glasses.

"Mr. Jacobson," said Dmitri.

"Put this boy in the car."

"*Wait*," said Dash. "Why can't he come with us? To Blumenthal's hotel?"

"That flea pit?"

Blumenthal stuck out his chest. "It is not a flea pit! I've stayed there many times."

"I'm sure you have. Just the same, I would have him at our hotel." He gestured to Dmitri.

Walt was awake now, sitting up, then kneeling. Dmitri leaned down to him, but Walt fended him off.

"Don't touch me! I can stand on my own!" He tried a couple of times but couldn't get off his knees. His face was the colour of a dolphin's belly. "Do I get a say in any of this?" he asked pathetically.

"No," said Houdini. "You need to rest, son. Drink a lemonade. Bess will look in on you."

"But I want to stay."

Houdini crouched in front of him. "Dashiel and I are lucky to have our Walter Gibsons, Walter Gibson. But you've done everything you needed to do today. And it is a fine thing to be looked in on by Mrs. Houdini. You'll be your old self in no time." He offered his hand and Walt took it. Houdini brought him to his feet. "Look at me, for instance. Healthy as a horse."

Walt went to where Jacobson was waiting by a circular saw.

"Walt!" Dash called. "Aw, just let him rest here!" he called to the adults.

"In all zees dust?" Pelletier gestured around at the machinery.

"Wait, hold on! Walt," he called again, and the other boy listened, his ear tilted up as he followed Jacobson out of the workshop. "Don't get on that train! Don't get on the morning train!"

But they were gone.

"Omigod—" He exhaled. "Thanks for backing me up!" he snarled at Blumenthal.

"I've backed you up plenty! But your friend is not well, and he'll be more comfortable at Houdini's hotel. Try to be a big boy about it."

"DON'T TALK TO ME LIKE I'M A KID!" Dash shouted. "I'm almost twelve years old, okay?" He sat down heavily in a chair. There were so many eyes on him. "I'm never going to see him again."

"I'm sure you'll see him after you've both had a good night's rest," said Houdini. "Too much excitement for everyone."

A terrible feeling flooded through Dash. "If this trick works, I'll never see him again."

Houdini and Pelletier exchanged looks and the master set-builder ushered his people back to their stations, leaving the two magicians alone with the boy.

"That is very possible," said Houdini. "But think how much worse it would be if you had never met at all."

"It would be better," Dash mumbled.

Houdini laid a hand on his shoulder. "No it wouldn't," he said. "In this life, a friend is a friend, no matter any of the other details. I won't be sad for you if the trick works, and you should not be sad for yourself. Or Walter Gibson. Now pull yourself together." He called for Pelletier.

The man appeared, drying his hands on a cloth. "*Maître?*"

"We're going to dry-run it, but I need the lights. Can you run them in the manner I wrote down for you?"

"*Absolument.*"

"What are you doing?" Dash asked.

"We're going to test the trick," said Blumenthal.

"No! You can't test it!"

"Everything has to be tested," said Houdini. "To ensure it will work."

"You can build it, but you can't test it on anyone. What if there's only, you know, like, one *charge* in it?"

"There must be more than one 'charge,'" said Blumenthal. "It sent you here, didn't it?"

"Yeah?" said Dash, his hands on his hips. "And what if you test it and send me home *now*. Then what do you do for your encore? When you *do* have an audience?"

Blumenthal clapped his hand to his forehead. "An audience. How am I going to get an audience with twenty-four hours' notice to come see a trick that doesn't work yet?"

"Ask Gluckman."

Blumenthal's face curdled. "I am not asking Gluckman for a favour."

"Who is Gluckman?" asked Houdini.

"My ex-manager."

"And owner of the Pantages," said Dash.

Houdini was smiling. "*That* Gluckman? Charlie Gluckman? I know Charlie! I'll give him a ring, why don't I?"

Blumenthal sighed. Houdini patted him on the back and then put his arm through Pelletier's.

"I do like your trick, Jacques. Let's hope it works on the first try. Although, I have the idea to light the bubble from a different angle. And how low and how far away could you place two fans?"

They walked off together. "I'm going back to the Prince of Wales and I'm getting Walt," said Dash. "I'll bring him to your hotel."

"You're like a dog with a bone," said Blumenthal. "You heard Harry. Don't you go over there and start more trouble."

"I don't *like* Jacobson," Dash snapped.

"Oh, don't be ridiculous."

"And I don't trust him neither. How did Mrs. Alphonsine find us? Huh? How do you know Jacobson isn't dropping Walt off at her door right now?"

"Because he isn't. Use your overactive imagination for better purposes. You can trust Walt with Sol. He's a good man."

"So you say, but you're in business with him now. I'm going to get Walt."

"Dash—" Blumenthal began, but he was already out the door.

He sped back to the hotel, keeping his head down. He waved at the desk clerk and went to install himself on the circular couch that enclosed a tree with long, thin hanging leaves. He shifted around until he found a view of the door and the elevators that was neither too open, nor too blocked by fronds. He was going to wait here until he saw Jacobson leave for the evening performance.

After an hour, he was still sitting there. He'd sagged against the back of the couch. He wondered if Houdini and Herman

Blumenthal were going to test the trick anyway. Maybe Blumenthal was already standing onstage at the Canon Theatre in 2011 with a bewildered look on his face . . .

Around six in the evening, the lobby became busier. He'd passed the time seeing how long he could go without blinking, repeating his name over and over in his head until it sounded like Martian, and once or twice, he thought about girls. Voices bounced off the floor and the gleaming white ceiling hung with chandeliers. Eventually, Marcel spotted him on his way into the dining room.

"Monsieur Woolf?" he said.

"Hi, Marcel," Dash said quietly.

"Where is everyone? You are coming for suppair?"

"I don't think so."

"'*Oudini* is better?"

"I guess." He wanted Marcel to leave him alone.

"You are coming for ze *bouillabaisse* again?"

"I don't know," said Dash. "Do you do it without the fish?"

Marcel smiled and messed his hair. Dash sank farther into the cushion below the lobby tree. He remembered flaking out on the couch in Alex's basement. Once a month, Alex's parents let him have Braindead Day, and that meant he had the whole day to play video games, read comic books, eat garbage, anything, and he could stay up as late as he wanted, too. The rest of the month, it was moderation, but Alex's parents thought Braindead Day was a good way to put a little craziness into the mix. They'd seemed like a happy family . . .

Back then, Dash's parents let him go every other month. Those were the best nights of the year. He and Alex were friends at school anyway, and it wasn't like they *didn't* see each other practically every day—and after school a lot of days as well—but those nights were just for them. No adults, no other kids. Nights of drinking pop and *eructating* the alphabet (they'd found the word in a dictionary), nights listening to the late-starting hockey games on the radio while playing Entrail Derby III: SkullSplash and eating so much popcorn and licorice that they'd have to sleep on top of their sleeping bags so they wouldn't be trapped with their own farts.

But you couldn't be friends with someone who wasn't there. There hadn't been a Braindead Day since his parents had split. Alex had emailed him a couple of times from Leiden, but Dash hadn't replied. Why? Was he going to go over there and sleep in his Dutch house in *Leiden* for one night? What would be the point? Alex had *wanted* to go with his mother. He'd had a choice, and he chose to leave. Obviously friendship wasn't that important to him.

He didn't want his mind to keep going like this, but he didn't have the energy now to shake off his thoughts. His guts felt like a fist.

It was nearly eight when Sol Jacobson entered the hotel. He hadn't been upstairs after all! Where had he been? Dash leapt up and made a beeline for him.

"Where's Walt?" he demanded.

Jacobson tried to sidestep him. "You're a pest."

"Where were you just now? Huh? You just drop him off?"

"What are you going on about?"

"Why aren't you at the show?"

"I don't watch every show," said Jacobson. He continued across the lobby.

Dash followed him to the elevators. "No, I'm sure you don't. You probably miss the ones when you have to go sneaking around doing stuff. I want to see Walt!"

Jacobson began pulling off his gloves. The arrow on the dial above the elevator showed it descending from the fifth floor. "He's resting. You go see the show. Harry left you a ticket. Anyway, you'll be on the train with Walter all day tomorrow."

"I will, will I?"

"Are you planning on staying?"

"No. I'm going on Houdini's train tomorrow afternoon. With Walt and Blumenthal."

"Walter will already be home by then. I guess you'll be wanting to change your ticket."

The elevator arrived. The operator greeted them both with a small bow. Dash held Jacobson back.

"I want him to come to Blumenthal's hotel."

"The house doctor has said Walter is to rest. I suspect your friend will prefer the feather pillows here anyway." He got into the elevator. Dash felt helpless. "Go to the show, whatever you are."

"What's *that* supposed to mean?"

"Harry does not believe in spirits, but I do. Go back to where you came from." The gate closed and the arrow on the dial showed the car moving upwards.

22

If Walt was safe and sound—or if he was on a train some-where—there was nothing Dash could do about it now. He decided he'd take a chance and leave the hotel. He'd never have another opportunity to see Houdini perform live, and he knew that Walt wouldn't want him to miss it.

He walked down to the Princess Theatre. It was just around the corner—he had been too excited two mornings ago to real-ize sooner that the car they'd gotten into was driving away from downtown. They could have just walked it.

The lights were dark in the empty lobby beyond the front doors. The lady at the booth still had the ticket Houdini had left him. An usher led Dash in and told him to stand in the back. It was too late to go all the way down to his seat.

The lights were low; it appeared that Houdini was between tricks. Then a spotlight came on and the curtains parted on a stage with nothing but a huge tank of water. Houdini emerged from the wings in a ribbed, white tank top and a pair of swimming trunks. His ankle was still bandaged and he limped on it. Even from the back of the theatre, Dash could see how weary he looked. His skin was sallow. But he was carrying on with the show.

"Ladies and gentlemen, to conclude my performance this evening, I am pleased to present to you the greatest death-defying act ever performed live on any stage: my Water Torture Cell." He gestured ominously to the menacing glass tank. "There is nothing supernatural about it, and I am prepared to offer the sum of one thousand dollars to any person who can prove that it is possible to get any air inside the Torture Cell when I am locked up in it in the regulation manner after it has been filled with water. If anything should go wrong when I am locked up in it, one of my assistants will come through the curtain and release the water from the tank, thereby saving my life. I hope that this will not be necessary. Now, with no further ado, I will request my stage assistants to lock me into the lid of the Torture Cell and lower me into it."

The tension in the room was terrible. Four men in black uniforms had rushed onto the stage wearing white gloves and they began to help the magician into his ankle harness. Houdini winced in pain as he was secured to the lid of the tank. The audience seemed to be leaning forward as one, drawn to the stage by the drama of this final effect, and as they watched, united in their worry and excitement, Dash scanned the edges of the theatre with his eyes. There were a couple of elderly patrons sitting in wheelchairs at the very back, and some ushers who had come in from the lobby to see the finale. Then Dash saw Blumenthal, his face glowing in light from the stage.

"And now, if my assistants will carefully lift the lid so that I am upside down, the cables will take care of the rest," said Houdini. The four men each took a corner and carefully hefted the small man into the air with his head hanging down, and then the cables attached to the lid pulled him even higher. He dangled above the mouth of the tank, his arms spread wide. "Ladies and gentlemen, I do hope I will see you again in a minute or so . . ."

Dash crossed behind the audience toward Blumenthal. He came up alongside him, and the man looked over briefly before returning his attention to the stage. Houdini was being lowered into the tank. Air bubbles escaped from his nose and ran up the side of the glass.

"Will it work?" Dash asked Blumenthal quietly.

"This? It better: he's my sponsor!"

"No. The Soap Bubble Vanish."

"I don't know," he replied. "Someone wouldn't let us test it."

"Don't you agree?"

Blumenthal's eyes ticked over Dash's face. "What does it matter if I agree? I am just a tiny cog in some larger machine. If you are to be believed."

"Are you on my side or not?"

"I am on the side of the angels. Should there be any."

Houdini was working away inside the tank. Dash couldn't watch.

"He doesn't look so good," he said.

"That man can take care of himself."

Suddenly, applause. They looked at the stage and Houdini was standing at the lip of it, dripping wet, his arms spread wide. The audience rose as one, all of them banging their hands together madly and hooting with delight.

Their view blocked, Dash and Blumenthal went to stand near one of the exits. Houdini looked as weak as a kitten.

"I saw Sol," Dash said over the continuing applause.

"How'd that go?"

"Not so well. I don't want him to put Walt on the morning train."

"How do you propose we fix that?"

"You can go get him in the morning. Jacobson can't say no to you."

Herman Blumenthal stubbed his finger into the middle of Dash's chest. "You're a big *macher*, aren't you? You think you can tell people what to do."

"Walter deserves to see the trick! He has to stay with us to the end."

"You mean *you*. That's what you mean every time you say 'us,' isn't it? Sometimes you seem a rather selfish young man."

The applause grew louder and drowned them out as Houdini took his final bows.

The only hotel Blumenthal could afford was considerably more modest than the Prince of Wales. The Butcher's Arms was a house on Rue Aylmer and the room was in the basement. The ceiling was at a height of five feet, which was fine for boys or gnomes, but when Blumenthal entered, he had to crouch down. A pipe dripping with cold condensation travelled the width of the room a foot below the ceiling, and a sink stuck out of one of the walls like a tongue in a face. Two shapeless beds sat along one wall, squatting in the dark: dirty little mounds. There was a large, scoop-like indentation in the middle of each bed, where the bodies of previous guests had settled.

"You hungry, kid?"

"Starving."

Blumenthal had an oily paper bag from which he pulled out a heel of salami and a couple things wrapped in waxed paper. It all smelled like the man's apartment had: smoky, greasy, fragrant with spice and rot.

"I brought supplies from home," he said. He laid out a few items on the little writing desk, including a cold cabbage roll and a few pickled herring, and put a couple of chocolate croissants alongside them. "You want a sandwich?"

"In a chocolate croissant?"

"All ends up in the same place." He tore two of the croissants open with his thumbs, and ripped the salami into rough chunks, which he apportioned between the two of them. He unwrapped the cabbage roll, revealing a long, grey pill of ground meat within. With his finger, he wiped smears of the meat into the middle of the split croissants. "Fish or no fish?" he asked Dash.

"How about I get the fish on the side?"

"Don't know what you're missing," said Blumenthal.

They ate in companionable silence. Dash's energy, which had been flagging under the weight of fearful thoughts, was returning. He could feel something aligning now; there were times when he sensed he was inside a track or a groove of some kind. It sometimes made the past feel familiar. He had this same feeling sometimes when he was playing tennis with his dad and the ball was coming to him and he knew where it was going to be, and all he had to do was plant his feet and grip the racquet with both hands. Movement did the rest.

Was time a kind of motion? If you closed your eyes, it seemed to stop. Maybe this was how he'd done so much here, in the past, if time was actually stopped where his parents were. Two thousand eleven was dark and unseeable, so there was no movement and no time there, just as there had been no time in the past he'd once imagined Houdini in. Only where his eyes were open, where he could be witness, did time appear to run.

"What is it with you and the faraway looks?" Blumenthal demanded. "You gonna finish that half or not?"

"I'm finishing it," Dash said. He was feeling stronger by the minute. "So do you want to hear my plan?"

"I don't know," said Blumenthal. "I might've had enough of your plans."

"This one involves you being my hero."

Blumenthal ran his tongue around his back teeth. "I'm listening."

"You have to talk Harry into getting off the train in Toronto."

"You heard Sol. Harry has a show that night."

"I can give him a good reason not to go on to Detroit. A night in Toronto is what he needs."

"What do you know that I don't?" Blumenthal asked him.

23

Early morning bloomed with its lambent light, and the streets were thick with people and cars. Dash felt he was fighting a tide as he walked quickly to Houdini's hotel. He went breathlessly into the lobby while Blumenthal waited outside. Dash took up his position on the circular couch again, this time out of view of the front doors, the elevators, *and* the restaurant. He caught his breath and nodded surreptitiously out the window to his accomplice.

Now Dash took a glance into the restaurant. When he was sure the coast was clear, he ran to the half-wall beside the teeming eatery, and crouched. There were more plants here, their leaves drooping over the wall. He scuttled to his left. Parting the leaves with his hands, he stuck his head in and peered around. He saw no one he recognized.

Dash went back to his position on the couch and signalled Blumenthal. The magician went directly to the desk and requested the clerk dial Sol Jacobson's room. Dash could hear both men from where he was sitting.

"He asks who it is," said the clerk.

"It's Herman Blumenthal."

"It's Herman Blumenthal, sir," the man said into the phone. He listened, then put his hand over the receiver. "Mr. Jacobson is unable to see you, sir."

"Tell him he needs to see me. There's the matter of his signature on the contract between myself and his client."

The clerk listened anxiously, nodding. "I see. Mr. Jacobson? The gentleman suggests the matter is of some importance. He refers to a contract. Yes, I will tell him." He covered the mouthpiece with his hand. "Mr. Jacobson says he is no longer employed in the capacity you refer to."

"Tell Mr. Jacobson that he has not submitted his resignation, therefore his signature is required."

Dash peeked around the couch. The clerk had grown hesitant. "Maybe sir would like to resolve this issue another time?"

"Tell him."

He brought the phone back to his ear. "I beg your pardon, sir, but the gentleman makes the point that your signature on this contract is still necessary and valid. Shall I send him up?" He pulled the earpiece away. Even Dash could hear Jacobson shouting.

"Sol!" Blumenthal called out. "Harry has offered to *donate* his services, he is so taken with our predicament! Isn't that wonderful?"

The clerk listened. "Ah," he said. "I will tell him, sir." He replaced the receiver. "Mr. Jacobson will be right down."

Dash kept as hidden as he could, but he slid around now until he could see the elevators. After a delay of a few minutes, he heard the gate open and the sound of expensive shoes clacking on the marble floor. He stuck his head around the foliage to see Jacobson proceeding across to Blumenthal, who'd installed himself by the front desk at the farthest point from the elevators. He stuck his hand out, and at that moment Dash strode as quickly and silently as possible toward the elevator, holding his hand up to signal to the attendant inside to wait. He stepped in, showed five fingers, and mouthed the number. The operator closed the gate and moved the lever to its Up setting. The elevator gave a lurch and whirred upwards, the floors passing in white and black whooshes before the gate.

"*Cinquième étage*," the operator said.

Dash exhaled and got out. Room 501. That was Houdini's suite. Dash knocked quietly on the door, but there was no answer. He knocked again. Nothing.

There were ten other doors on the floor. He stood in the middle of the hallway hoping that someone he didn't recognize would come out of one of the rooms so he could rule at least one out. But the hallway was as quiet as a mausoleum.

There was a door to a stairwell at the end. Dash slipped through it to stand on the landing. He kept the door open just six inches and filled his lungs and belted out, as loud as he could:

"WALTER GIBSON! CAN YOU HEAR ME, WALT?"

Then he let the stairwell door close. He pressed his ear

against it and listened. At first he thought the sound of his heart under his shirt was footsteps approaching along the carpet, but no—and then there was nothing else. He was about to give up when he heard a very light knock on the door he was hiding behind.

He opened it a crack. "I thought that was you," said Walt. "Whyint you just knock?"

"You're here."

"Wheredya think I was? Playing the ponies?"

"I thought . . . maybe . . ."

"Maybe what?"

"Nothing," said Dash. "Just glad to see you."

"Yeah," said Walt, making a queer face. "Nice to see you too."

He led Dash back down the hall. He seemed perfectly fine. In fact, his eyes were practically shining, like he'd just woken up from a refreshing sleep.

"We don't have time," Dash said. "You have to come with me now."

"Why? Train's not for another two hours."

"You're not getting on that train. Blumenthal is downstairs, distracting Jacobson so I can get you out! Grab your things!"

"Oh, I'm fine," Walter said laconically. "I don't know what you're so worried about."

"What's going on with you?"

"Nothing's going on. I'm just not coming."

"Did you take a page out of *his* book?"

Walt squared himself. "What's that supposed to mean?"

"Well, Jacobson doesn't think anything of walking out on *his* friends."

"Hey, I got into a lot of trouble for you, Dash. I haven't walked out! I'm sick and Sol Jacobson is the only one who cares. And anyway, I'm eating fresh baguette with preserves and they put a radio in the room as well."

"What is wrong with you, Walt? You look like someone knocked you on the head."

"They gave me some medication. I feel better."

"What medication?"

"I had a spoonful of Mentho-Kreoamo, one of Broncil, and a tonic in a tea, which was bitter."

"Come with me, Walt. We won't have to ride with pigs, I promise. And Houdini will buy us chocolate if we ask him, I'm sure of it!"

"Every time I follow one of *your* plans, Dash, they don't work out so well."

"They will this time. And this is the last time, I promise."

They took the stairs, Walt with his crumpled rucksack under his arm, and came out onto McGill College Avenue, as Dash and Blumenthal had arranged. Jacobson would already be heading back to his room. After waiting for a moment in the shadows, Dash saw Blumenthal come around the corner, waving them on.

"Let's go!" he called, and they did.

In plain daylight, Rue Aylmer wasn't as sinister as it had

seemed the night before, but it still didn't feel like a place where a kid should be walking alone, even at nine in the morning. There were already whiskery men sitting in their coats on stoops with stubby-necked bottles of beer, or paper bags that clearly had bottles in them. They were rolling and smoking their own cigarettes from pouches with brand names like Tik Tak and Prince Albert Crimp Cut.

Dash and Walt entered the lobby of the Butcher's Arms, trying to avoid the cracked tiles where grime had gathered. No elevator operator. The desk clerk didn't even look at them when they came in. They took the side stairs.

Blumenthal had left his door open.

Walt looked around the room with distaste. "This is what I left the Prince of Wales for?"

"We're only here for a while. Just relax," said Blumenthal.

"What's the plan, though?"

"We're going on the three o'clock," said Dash. "Houdini's train. Herman is going to try to get him to stop in Toronto."

"Now I'm Herman?"

"He already agreed not to," said Walt. "He promised Sol. I heard him."

"He has to!" said Dash. "If he gets all the way to Detroit, Walt—"

"Then *what*?" interrupted Blumenthal.

"Nothing," said Dash. "Then he doesn't get to see the trick he helped invent."

*

At eleven thirty, they sent Blumenthal out for hamburgers. And malts.

As he was leaving, Dash called, "And see if you can get yesterday's paper! For Walt!"

"Oh, I already read it," said Walt. "Sol had one."

"But to keep," said Dash.

"I don't need one," Walt said. "And I clipped the article we're in already."

"Hold on. You clipped the paper?"

"Yes," said Walt.

"You have it right now?"

"I have it in my pocket."

"Take it out," said Dash. "I want to see it."

Walt reached into his pants pocket and removed a folded piece of newsprint. He put it on the bed and it began to unspring, like a magically blooming white rose. Dash took his out as well.

"Well, wait, int yours half a page?"

"Yes," said Dash, unfolding the piece of newsprint he'd been given at the Canon Theatre. "But it was once a full page, wasn't it? Look," he said, "your first fold is in half crossways!"

The two of them stood over the two pages, one crisp and white as steam, the other worn and browned and soft to the touch. The upper half of Walt's paper echoed every fold in Dash's.

"How can we both have the same piece of newspaper?"

"We can't. We can't, so we don't. I have mine and you have yours. Mine is from 2011, I know, because that's where I got it and I've lived there my whole life and I'm not crazy enough to have thought this all up."

"You're a *little* crazy," offered Walt.

"I know . . . but I didn't make you up. Or Blumenthal, and everyone knows Houdini existed. I couldn't have invented what *your* Toronto is like. The smell of smoke everywhere, different sounds, sounds I'd never heard before. How could I have imagined them? So if 1926 is *now* for you and 2011 is now for *me*, maybe all the nows are happening all at once and there are an infinity of newspapers out there, each one from its own now."

"You lost me at smells," said Walt.

"And yet," said Dash, brandishing the old newspaper, "this has to be yours. If the folds are identical. That newspaper you got from Jacobson this morning is somehow the one I have."

"But you said it was a boy who gave you the envelope."

"You're ninety-six in 2011. Maybe you're backstage too, Walt. In a rocking chair."

When Blumenthal came back with the food, they showed him the clippings, still laid out on the bed. It took him a moment, and he had to look a couple of times, but then he said, "Holy . . ."

Dash wouldn't have to worry about him being a non-believer anymore.

After they had eaten, Blumenthal relaxed in a chair and lit a Phillie.

"I wish you wouldn't," said Dash. "Walt's still under the weather."

"I like the smell," Walt said.

"Anyway, they're no good for you."

"What? This?" Blumenthal turned the end of the cigar around and looked at it. "Smoke strengthens your lungs! It's a tonic to the nerves." He was vanishing french fries studded with salt. "But do tell. What prognostications have you for this prestidigitator? Since you know so much about what is unseen and unknown."

"Well, you find someone," said Dash. "A lady."

"Do I? I don't think any ladies are thinking of marrying Blumenthal—with his best man, a squirrel. A girl maybe. I'll settle for a girl."

"And you change your name too."

"I change my name." He pulled his head back. "I hope it's to Rockefeller."

"Blumenthal the Believer."

Herman Blumenthal narrowed his eyes. "You know, I like that. But . . ." He looked down at the floor and then back up at Dash. "Never mind. Maybe I like it."

"You like it," said Walt, staring at his face. "And you should have seen your face when he said someone was actually gonna marry you."

Blumenthal swatted at him, laughing. "You're a card, Mister Gibson. You should have your own act."

*

They resolved to stay in the hotel room until it was time to take the train. There was no point in being out. *At large*, as Blumenthal put it. For a while, everyone fell into a post-hamburger coma, lolling in chairs like lions lunching on an impala.

Then they rallied a little. Dash stretched his arms and ran on the spot, which is something he had only done in gym class. Blumenthal collected the garbage.

"How'd it work out with Gluckman?" Dash asked. "Did Houdini set it all up?"

"Gluckman knows we're coming," he muttered.

Dash laughed, a little unkindly. "You can't even get away from him. You have to do the trick in his building."

"It's a small world. You run into people. If I have to work with him, then I will. But I won't trust him."

Walter was beginning to droop again. He went back to the bed. By this time Houdini's matinee had begun. Dash wondered if Jacobson was watching from the wings. How long would it take him to forgive Houdini for being Houdini? Soon, Jacobson was probably going to see *exactly* what his friendship with Erich Weiss would cost him. Unless somehow Dash was able to stop Houdini from making his appointed date with his appointed destiny.

At two, they woke Walt and collected their things. It was a short walk and the boys' rucksacks were half empty anyway. Blumenthal carried Walt's. They heard the steely jostling of the trains before they saw the station, and then they came upon it, the huge stone face stretching down two blocks, doors at the corners. The sounds of voices and trains inside the station bounced off the high stone walls.

The clock in the middle of the open concourse said it was two thirty. They had half an hour before the train departed. Dash had a feeling that Sol Jacobson would have his eye—or others'—out for them. He was sure the man knew they had missed their ten o'clock on purpose.

Blumenthal led them down a corridor, away from the platforms. "Sit'eer." He indicated an iron bench with wood slats. "I'll be back in two minutes. Gimme your tickets."

"No way," said Walt.

"You can't get on the three o'clock with tickets stamped for ten. I have to exchange them."

Dash passed him his, and then they both stared at Walt. "Holy cow, Walt, what's he gonna do? Take the train three times on his own?"

"All right." Walter passed the ticket over.

"Don't move," said Blumenthal. He went to the end of the corridor and turned out of sight.

"Well, that'll be the last we'll see of him," Walt joked.

"He did rescue us from juvie, remember."

They sat in silence, watching for him. He was gone for longer than two minutes, but then he came jauntily around the corner with a red packet of thin cigars in his hand. He had just tapped one out when his face changed and the cigar fell from his fingers. He broke into a run.

Instinctively, both boys leapt up, as a voice behind them roared in triumph: "AHA!" Two thick hands with hair sprouting from their knuckles came down like hammers on each of their shoulders. "Here you are *again*!"

They turned to see the owner of the knuckles. Officer Blackwell. Dash noticed his bruise wasn't exactly healing. It was the colour of an eggplant now.

Herman Blumenthal skidded to a stop in front of them. "Getcher hands off these boys!"

"A regla coupla tramps, aren't they?" He shook them. "Howdja get out of Mrs. Alphonsine's hotel anyway?" He looked like he wanted to kill them.

"*I* sprung 'em!" said Blumenthal. "Now let go!"

"And who are you?"

"I'm their father."

"Sure you are. You look a right father to scuts like these."

"Let us go!" Dash shouted, yanking against him.

"Which train were you family of hobos all planning to hop this fine afternoon?"

"We have tickets," said Blumenthal. He held them up to the man.

Blackwell let go of Dash to take them. "You think you're all just going to go home now, eh?" he said. He studied the tickets and then folded them roughly and put them into his breast pocket.

"Hey, hold on, those belong to us!"

"We'll see how their value holds up against the cost of the boys' grub and lodging at the house on the hill. Maybe you'll *all* have to do a spell there."

"Please," said Walter. "You don't understand."

Blackwell got his cuffs out and snapped them on his wrist.

"Leave him alone!" cried Dash. There was a small crowd forming, blue uniforms scattered throughout it like dark berries among leaves. And there was another one of those men with a plain black ring on his lapel. Dash saw it and felt himself relax. They had the same eyes, but in different faces.

"He won't be alone," said Blackwell, producing a second pair of cuffs. "The stationmaster's in his office, dying to meet you. And you too, sir! Your boys have earned themselves quite a name!" He grasped the chain connecting them and pulled Walt and Dash together like a brace of dead partridges.

"Do you need shackling?" Blackwell called over his shoulder, whereupon Blumenthal the Believer began to follow solemnly behind.

24

They waited on a hard, wooden bench inside the stationmaster's office. Three men in guard uniforms stalked the space in front of them, discussing the situation with each other, and occasionally shooting their prisoners a disdainful glance. Officer Blackwell was behind a frosted door in the rear wall with the stationmaster.

"We're in major crud," said Dash. The clock on the wall showed it was creeping up on 2:45.

"Crud?"

"Poop. We're up to our necks in poop. We're going to miss the train."

"We'll get another train."

"This is the only train that matters anymore."

"Stop complaining," said Blumenthal. "And let me do the talking."

Five more minutes passed. The train was leaving in ten. Dash let out a groan.

One minute after that, the door in the back flew open, and out strode a colossus in a dark blue uniform with a stiff cap riding high on his head. He had to bend down under the door frame. The stationmaster. How excellent that he was this large and appeared so unhappy.

Behind him, two men in suits, the policeman Blackwell, and a woman in a grey wool skirt appeared, jostling in the doorway. The lady was holding a clipboard against her chest. Another official whose jurisdiction was children.

"These are they?" the stationmaster asked.

"Indeed," said Officer Blackwell. He had a proud look on his face, like the cat who ate the canary, as Dash's mother would have said. By the door, a small cadre of station guards and police officers had gathered and they were standing in a semicircle, looking in. "I knew there was something amiss when I ran into them Wednesday."

"Thank you for a job well executed . . ."

"Call me Eudorus," said Officer Blackwell.

"Eudorus. Well, a job well done indeed," he said. He went to the outer door in a single stride and shut it hard, crowding out the onlookers. Dash heard at least one nose conk the door. "In any event, I will take it from here."

"Will you need my name and badge number?" Blackwell asked eagerly.

"Of course, of course," the stationmaster said. He nodded to a man behind him. "Give him a penny or two." Another man stepped forward and put one coin into the constable's hand.

He looked down at it, then up at the stationmaster. "Just doing my job," he said with a disappointed-but-smiling expression. He removed the cuffs and put them back on his belt. "See you around . . . boys."

Blackwell left, and the stationmaster's three prisoners watched him turn his large, sturdy frame in their direction. He trod toward them on powerful legs. The man's body seemed to blur in Dash's vision and he felt dizzy for a moment; a pang of nausea shot through him. The stationmaster's voice sounded far away.

"Well," it said. "We have something very curious here, now don't we?"

"Sir, please. This is a misunderstanding," said Walt. "It's important that you let us go. Right away, in fact."

"Important? Right away? It must also be imperative."

"Yes, yes, it is. It is *very* imperative."

"Must you go IMMEDIATELY?" he roared. He leaned in and his eyes seemed as large as billiard balls.

"Sir," said Blumenthal, rising confidently, but the stationmaster put a hand out and Blumenthal bumped into it.

"You will go to a place of my choosing," the man said quietly now to all of them. "Because this is my house, and you have beset it recklessly; you have besmirched it. You set *upon it* a herd of wild animals!"

"They were only pigs," said Walt quietly. "Harmless pigs . . ."

"SILENCE!" The man's upper lip thinned. He pushed Walt back against the bench with a giant index finger. "I will have you *both* in Mrs. Alphonsine's home for—"

He didn't finish his sentence: there was instead a tremendous flash of colour and sound. A holler of red and white and black with a blur of freckles within it. The stationmaster's eyes retreated and became as still as a photograph and to Dash's astonishment Walt was frozen in the air. Beside him, Blumenthal's mouth was stilled in an expression of shock, and everyone in the office had turned into statues. It was suddenly silent.

Oh, Dash heard himself say in his own head, and then a disembodied voice announced: "*Ladies and gentlemen, it is one thing to vanish without a trace, but it is quite ano . . . ther . . . to—*" And it broke off. And Walt landed on the stationmaster's chest with a resounding thud amid cries and protests.

"Go!" Walt shouted to Blumenthal through a cyclone of limbs. "Get out of here! Get him home!"

Then Dash was on his feet, his legs working furiously. He grabbed Blumenthal by the front of the shirt and the two of them tore the door open. Twenty faces jolted in surprise and then parted and let them through. They were on the station's concourse, flailing, and they stopped and looked back: Walt was throwing himself around inside the office. Dash stumbled backwards, astonished.

"We have to go in there and get him," said Blumenthal, straining forward at the back of the crowd.

"No," said Dash.

"You'll leave your friend in—"

"Well, I see you are forced to hoof it," said a voice.

They spun to see Harry Houdini in a wooden wheelchair. Standing behind was Bess in a black fur ruff and a rather wonderful hat with flowers and draped lace. Houdini was wearing a pair of heavy steel sunglasses. He took them off.

"Bess, these are the other gentlemen I was telling you about."

She held out her hand and they each took it in turn, anxiously, giving their names. Dash was distracted by the silence behind him: the door to the stationmaster's office was closed again.

"Walt is in there," said Blumenthal, hooking his thumb toward the stationmaster's door.

"He is? Well, we'll have to get him, then. The train is about to leave." He attempted to get out of the chair, but the instant he came into contact with the palm of Bessie's hand, he sat right down again.

"Behave," she said. "And put your sunglasses back on. You have to rest your eyes. You know what Dr. LaFleur said about too much light."

"But we may have to effect a rescue, missus."

Sol Jacobson appeared behind Bess. Dash locked eyes with him.

"It would seem Master Woolf prevented Master Gibson from making his 10 a.m. train."

"Well, good thing they ran into us, isn't it, Sol? They'd better make this one."

"Excellent," he said sourly.

So Sol was still in Harry's employ, Dash noted. What could that mean?

Houdini's driver, Dmitri, was coming into the station through the glass doors. The light, reflecting off the kiosks, the floor, and the high windows made Dash feel like he'd tumbled into a kaleidoscope.

"Come with me," Sol said to Dmitri. The driver saluted his boss.

"You'll bring him to the train, Dmitri?"

"Yes, *maestro*, the boy will be on the train."

The two men strode toward the stationmaster's door.

"Sometimes people think we're brothers," said Houdini, "but we didn't even grow up in the same state."

"Come on now," said Bess, her face a mask of exasperation, "we've five minutes to make the train!"

"Well, then," said Houdini, rising out of the chair, "we had better run for it. Leave the wheelie, my darling! We'll telegraph the hotel tomorrow to come pick it up. *Quai* Seven!"

Dash and Blumenthal each grabbed one of Houdini's suitcases; Houdini, over his wife's protestations, tucked one under his arm and grabbed two others by their handles.

"I cannot carry you as well, my love," he said to her, and started off toward the *quai*.

She came after, with heavy, angry footfalls. Dash cast a single backwards glance—what choice did he have now? He'd have to trust Jacobson.

The first-class steward looked at Herman Blumenthal's clothes, and then the expensive suitcase he was carrying, and then his clothes again. "They're *his*," said Blumenthal, holding up Houdini's things. "Can you just put them on the train?"

Houdini rushed up behind. "They're with me," he said, and the steward's face seemed to be paralyzed between two expressions.

"Are you Mr. Harry—?"

"Yes. Take our things, will you?"

Bess went past and tucked a dime into the man's vest pocket.

"Be quick, youngster," she said to Dash.

Houdini took the first empty compartment. "That's not ours," said Bess, but he'd needed to sit down. He was winded.

Bess went ahead with Blumenthal.

"Don't get old," Harry said to Dash, and he laughed good-naturedly.

"You're not old."

"Not as old as some, no."

"Sir?"

"Whatever it is you know, young Dashiel, keep it to yourself."

"I wish you believed me."

Houdini rested himself against the back of the train seat. "I do believe you, Master Woolf."

"You do?"

"Yes." He closed his eyes. "I even know why the trick works. I don't purport to know *how*, but I think I understand why. You see, if your Blumenthal performs the vanish tonight, it will be the first time it is ever performed. But if you step inside it, it will be the second time it has been performed on *you*." He opened his eyes and looked into Dash's. They were like two small glowing coals. "That is a paradox: it's perfectly impossible. But it is a paradox that somehow works. Both sides of it, however contradictory, are true. And when you step into the trick, Dashiel, you are like a battery that turns it on."

"Come see it, then!"

Houdini's expression shifted. He looked frightened now. "No." Dash lowered his head. "I have a show in six and a half hours, Dashiel. How can I stop in Toronto?"

"You've gone this far," he replied. "Why not see it through?"

"I wish I could. But I won't disappoint my public. Now, let us talk of more interesting things."

"Like what?"

"Like, when will we start visiting the moon?"

"A long time from now."

"When I am old."

Dash looked away. "There will be rockets that go way past the moon too."

"How far?"

"They're still going."

"Come on now, what else?" The conductor was blowing his whistle out on the platform.

"Electric cars. Instant photographs. You'll be able to put your eyeglasses right into your eyes. Watches get really interesting. And people live longer."

Houdini smiled at him and his eyes sparkled. Dash looked up, and Sol was standing on the other side of the door, one hand clamped down on Walt's shoulder.

Houdini leaned forward and patted Dash's cheek. "I enjoyed meeting you, Master Woolf. Now, take my advice: work hard! And if you can, make others happy." He rose to open the door. Sol was about to protest, but Houdini said, "I know. This is not their car. Go along, both of you. Mr. Blumenthal will join you in your compartment. I would like to get to know my business associate better."

Dash passed Herman Blumenthal in the passage. "Get him to the theatre!" he rasped at him. "He says he believes me now!"

He and Walter stepped down to the platform just as a voice boomed: "TORONTO! QUAI SEPT. EN VOITURE, S'IL VOUS PLAÎT. LE TRAIN PARTIS. TORONTO. PLATFORM SEVEN! ALL-LLL ABOARD! THE DOORS ARE CLOSING!"

Their car was two doors away. The conductor whistled again and the wheels on the rail scraped into motion. Dash and Walt jumped up on a step. Another agent, this one an older man with a gentle smile, unhooked the metal chain and let them through. He took their tickets and saw them to their seats. Through the windows, the posts fixed in the platform between tracks seven and eight began to move.

The train was leaving the station.

In their compartment a mother and daughter faced each other by the door. The girl had long blond hair with a red ribbon in it. She was six or seven. They all greeted each other politely, and Dash and Walter took the window seats and sat facing each other. They were motionless, still half in shock, wondering if their luck was going to turn sour again. The train picked up speed and the squealing of the wheels gave way to chugging and clattering.

Dash was staring backwards into the retreating train station. "That's it," he whispered to Walt. "We're going."

"Will he come? To see the trick?"

They watched the city thin outside the window.

"I don't know," said Dash.

"You should be careful with him. I mean Blumenthal. He's liable to send you to Pompeii."

Dash sighed. "Thank you for what you did back there, Walt. I'm really glad you were with me here. I don't think I would have been able to get through this without you."

Walter hid a proud smile.

As the train swayed west out of the city, the little girl kept pointing out things of interest to her mother, objects in the compartment, the landscape beyond the window. Dash smiled at her.

"May I ask you a question?" she said.

"Sure."

"Was that Houdini? In the station?"

"Oh . . . well, I suppose it might have been."

"Houdini was in Montreal! Mama brought me to see him."

"Ah. Did you like the show?"

"I thought it splendid!"

"We also saw him."

"Oh, how very lucky for you." Her mother was smiling down at her. "Did *you* enjoy the show?"

"Very much."

"Did your brother like it?"

Dash looked over at Walt. His eyes were closed and his head was nodding against the window in time to the movement of the train.

"Yes," said Dash. "He liked it very much."

25

The afternoon sun fell on the water and the fields and the woods, and reports of light went off here and there like blasts of sound, white and yellow suddenings of light. Dash let it calm him and lull him, and he put his head against the window and looked through his own face, floating over everything.

He closed his eyes. He had the impression of movement and shapes as shadows crossed over his lids. He felt the tall, plush seat-back against him, the soft end of the armrest under his elbow. The sound of the train joined itself to the pulse in his temple.

He didn't think he'd sleep. He was too excited and worried. But when he opened his eyes again, the world in the window was different. Not in detail, but in light. A deeper light. It was six o'clock in the evening now and it would be dark soon. The little girl slept against her mother and the lady's eyes were closed as well.

Dash noticed Walt was awake. He was looking at the girl sadly. "You okay?" Dash asked.

Walt turned his gaze to Dash, like he was coming out of a dream. "I guess we must be most of the way . . ."

"What can you see?"

"Fields."

Dash changed sides, sitting beside Walt so he could see the night coming in the westerly distance.

"What are you going to do as soon as you get home?" Walt asked.

"Hug my mum. What about you?"

"Sleep for three days. I'll hug my mum too, though." He looked back over at the mother and daughter. "Probably even Dee Dee."

"Do you like having a sister?"

"Most of the time," Walt answered. "Not all the time." He laughed at a private memory.

Dash had always wondered what it would feel like to have a sibling. "Do you have a best friend?"

"Sure. Peter. Christopher and me are good friends. Martin *thinks* he's my best friend—"

"I only have one," Dash said. "But he moved away with his mother."

"His dad died?"

"No. They got divorced."

"Oh. Whydee go with his mother?"

"She got a job somewhere else."

"But his dad stayed in Toronto?"

"Uh-huh."

"So what?" said Walter. "Won't he come back and visit eventually?"

"I guess so. But they moved to a place called *Leiden*."

"Holland?"

"Anyway," Dash said, looking sidelong at him, "he'll visit, I guess. But we won't be friends anymore."

Walter nodded soberly. If Dash had said something like that in front of either of his parents, one of them—at least—would have given him a lecture on not being so negative. But Walt understood. Dash and Alex would still know each other, but when you can't call someone up and meet them on the corner in ten minutes, it's not the same.

They watched the towns speed by along the lake, lulled by the world in the window like something seen on a stage. Soon, in the distance, they saw night over Toronto. They watched the city expand in it. Then Dash sat back and a deeper dark swelled in the sky.

"Omigod," Dash said.

Walt pulled his head away from the scene in the window. "What?"

"I forgot to tell you something. You have to remember this. There are going to be *superheroes*."

"Superheroes."

"Cartoon superheroes printed in little magazines called comic books. They haven't been invented yet, but they're coming. They're gonna be awesome. You should get some when they come out."

"When are they coming out?"

"I don't remember."

"Anything else?"

"Get Mickey Mantle's rookie card! He's a baseball player." He saw Walt memorize *Mick-ey Man-tle*. He told him about Superman and Batman, and about Donald Duck and Little Lulu and The Spectre. "Tell your grandkids to buy *Giant-Size X-Men*, number one. And keep it safe," he said. "And you have to grab *Action Comics* when it comes out—"

The city drew closer quickly. The train slowed as it pulled into Union Station.

The lady roused her daughter. "Goodbye," Dash said to them as they made their way out into the aisle. It was thronging with people eager to be home.

"What do you say, Beatrice?"

"Goodbye, boy," the girl said to him. She made a tiny bow to Walt. "Goodbye, other boy."

Blumenthal waited for them on the platform. Dash rushed over to him.

"Is he coming? Did you ask him?"

"You're lucky I'm such a good negotiator," Blumenthal said. "I didn't just get Harry to agree to come; Jacobson is coming too. They're going to postpone the Detroit show!"

So good old Sol had come through as well! Dash threw his arms around him. "Oh! You're amazing! Where is he?"

"Sol says they telegraphed ahead for a car. They'll be there. What's wrong with him?" he asked. Walt was coming down the train steps slowly. "Are you okay?"

"I'm exhausted," said Walt.

"Walt, Houdini's coming to the show!"

The boys allowed their chaperone to take all the bags and they walked down the stairs into the arrivals concourse.

"Do you think your parents will let you come and see the trick?" Dash asked. "Wouldn't you like to see it?"

"I can ask," said Walt, "but I'll probably be grounded until I'm forty now."

"Your mother might let you. Maybe she can let you out of the house for just an hour? We're going to do it at *eleven*. That's not too late! An' it's a Saturday night!"

They walked along under the main hall and then climbed the marble stairs with the polished brass railing into the hubbub and announcements. Dash looked behind him to see Blumenthal fumbling up with the rucksacks and his bags.

"Where is the, you know, the trick?" Dash asked him.

"It's being delivered separately to the theatre."

They stepped onto the gleaming floors of the station's main hall, and immediately they heard Walt's name being called. Dash saw Mrs. Gibson parting the crowd with her hands.

"Oh, Walter! Sweetheart!"

He ran to his mother. Mr. Gibson brought up the rear with a flat, suffering face. The man was so angry he could barely speak. He waited for his wife and son to finish their reunion and then he gestured for them to come.

"Wait a second," Dash said, and he ran over to them. "Mr. Gibson, Mrs. Gibson? This was all my fault. I talked him into going with me. He's such a . . . a great guy, you know? He couldn't refuse me when I told him I really needed his help!"

Mr. Gibson pulled Walt beside him and stepped toward Dash. His face was inches away. "It's up to you what you do with your own life, but you put my only son in the way of trouble? Don't think I'll forget it!"

"Walt?" said Dash. "Walt? I'm sorry if I got you into trouble. Okay?"

"Sorry if you got him into trouble," Mr. Gibson sneered.

Walter pushed his father aside and came forward. "Wait, I almost forgot!" He took a small paper bag out of his pocket and shook its contents out into his hand: two small, black rings. He gave one to Dash. "I got them out of a vending machine in the Prince of Wales," he said. "I thought we could each have one. As souvenirs."

Dash looked at his friend's offering and he felt his spirits sinking. "Give it to me tonight," he said, trying to hand his back.

But Walter closed Dash's fingers around the ring.

"In case I don't make it," he said.

Then Walter's mother put her hand on his shoulder, and the three of them walked out into the cold, October air beyond the station doors.

Blumenthal flagged down a cab, and he and Dash got into the back. It was about nine o'clock on a Saturday evening in Toronto. The heavy black vehicle bumped over the cobblestone of downtown as it went up Yonge Street and passed by Wellington and by King.

These were the streets his father had been telling him about when they'd been waiting in line at the Canon Theatre, and Dash had only been half listening. This was the old heart of the city, full of theatres and restaurants, brownstone arcades and white-columned bank buildings facing each other over the busy thoroughfare. It was very much alive now. Little tongues of fire licked up the glass lamps atop their posts along the road. There were people walking arm-in-arm among constellations of gaslight, and the little fragile-looking black cars tooted in and out of traffic. The square, black tops of the Fords were echoed in the round, too-high top hats on the men. It was no wonder no one wore them anymore. They were just silly. Although, he had to admit, they were also kind of cool.

Everyone was out. It was the place to be, Yonge Street. Maybe there were other places to be—in his own time, there certainly were—but here, this was it. Yonge and King Streets, Yonge and Queen, Yonge and Dundas. Downtown.

It had begun to snow.

26

Blumenthal directed the driver north. When they came up level with the Pantages, he pointed him onto Victoria Street behind the theatre and had him drop them off at the stage door.

He knocked, then turned around to Dash. "Don't say anything!"

The door opened. The man who had chased him off the stage with a flashlight five days earlier stood at the bottom of a set of stairs. "Herman," he said. "I see you made good time."

"Hello, Charlie. This is the boy I was telling you about."

Dash offered him his hand. "Dashiel Woolf."

Gluckman didn't remember him. Thank goodness. "Nice to meet you. Any friend of Herman's . . ."

"Enough with the charm," Blumenthal said, stepping into the foyer. "We have a problem."

"Another one?"

"Houdini is coming."

"WHAT? When?"

"Tonight."

"He said nothing to me about that."

Dash stepped in. "He decided on the train. Is there a problem?"

"Well, I didn't think we were going to have an audience," said Gluckman.

"You didn't invite anyone?" Blumenthal was livid.

"Why would I invite anyone, Herman? I'm not your manager anymore! Remember, *you* fired *me*! I'm doing a favour for Harry. Giving you fifteen minutes on my stage, with my lights, and that's it. *Audience*."

"You need an audience, Herman," said Dash.

"I told you to keep quiet."

"This your new manager?" said Gluckman. "I see you traded up." Dash wanted to stomp on the man's foot. "What a head for business you have, Herman. *I'll* find you an audience." His lip curled. "For old times' sake."

He let them into his theatre.

"Where is he?" Dash whispered to Blumenthal. "Where's Houdini?"

"He'll be here, Mr. Manager. Go get yourself fixed up. Someone backstage will iron your suit for you."

After the paying customers filed out of the Pantages' eight o'clock show, a different kind of crowd began to form outside the theatre. It was ten now, and the snow was coming down hard. Men and women, many in shabby coats, some with children, were waiting on the sidewalk. A few of the women carried baskets covered with white cloths.

"So this is my audience," Blumenthal said gloomily, staring out the door from the lobby. "Fur-cutters and tobacco salesmen. And their big women with baskets fulla kishka."

"What did you want on two hours' notice?" asked Gluckman.

"These people *like* magic," Dash said. "Look at them. Don't you think they could use some? And I bet they'll talk about it afterwards."

The crowd continued to swell on the sidewalk. Blumenthal stood far back in the dark, his shirtsleeves rolled up past his elbows. At ten thirty, they opened the doors. Quickly the seats filled up. Gluckman had got the whole of Kensington in on short notice: there were women with kerchiefs and children in little square suits; grandfathers with old black hats; and girls in long pigtails. A pale, bearded man who looked too young to be a father was playing with his three sons in the front row. There were many languages flying around. Dash recognized a little of the German and the Yiddish. There were other languages too: Russian? he thought. Chinese?

He and Blumenthal returned behind the curtains, where men with ladders were scattered over the stage now, working.

"So where's Harry Houdini?" asked Gluckman, unimpressed.

"He'll be here," said Dash.

Dash tuned the men out. All of his thoughts were for Walter.

What chance was there that his parents would let him come? Had they said their final goodbyes in the crowded hall of Union Station? He knew Walt would try his best, but it was getting late. Gluckman's audience was restless.

Men lowered cables from the ceiling through pulleys. The curtains remained closed.

"Where is your jacket?" Blumenthal said.

"I forgot to get it."

"Go now, then! The pretty girl in the steaming room already did it, I saw." He was doing up his tie in the wings. His shirt was clean. He looked good.

"I'm going outside."

"Where to?"

"Just to get some air."

"This is for you! Don't run off."

"I won't."

"Ten minutes."

Ten minutes. Perhaps somehow, Walt would make it.

Dash grabbed his clean jacket from the laundry office. Hannah, who'd taken the wrinkled shirt off him, now helped him back into it. She helped him put his cufflinks on properly too.

"I saw Herman," she said, a little shyly.

"Yes. He . . . seemed happy to see you too."

"Oh!" She pushed her lips out a little to keep from smiling. "Such a nice man. And so talented!"

He thanked her for the pressed shirt and left through the

stage door, turning the corner toward Yonge Street. The snow was still falling. It gathered on the sidewalk in fluffy clusters like dandelions gone to seed. They puffed away from his feet as he walked.

Out front of the theatre, a few stragglers were arriving late for the free show. Dash went back to the front of the theatre and stood under the marquee lights. He tried to look through the falling snow to the other side, but all the electric light turned the air to fog. *Eaton Centre over there. Dundas Square just up the sidewalk. The streetcars are red.* More latecomers filed in, but Walt was not among them.

Gluckman was in the window of the door behind him, waiting to close the house. When Dash turned back to the road, he felt dizzy. He heard that voice again: *The circle of life*, it said, and applause sounded distantly. He saw a flickering in the snowbound road, like lightning through clouds, headlamps and street lamps breaking through the weather. Gluckman opened one of the doors and called to him.

"Hurry up!"

"What about Houdini?"

"He got here an hour ago. He wouldn't come in until the house lights were down. His wheelchair is in the aisle, third row. Now get going."

Dash ran to the dim hallway that led backstage. He was panting, frightened, but also excited. It dawned on him suddenly that if he *was* going home, it would be mere minutes from now. He stopped in the wings and saw Blumenthal standing out there on the stage, lit by candles. The magician bowed slightly to him. Dash pulled his suit jacket down hard on his shoulders and nodded his readiness.

Gluckman was in the opposite wing. He pulled the curtains open and dimmed the house lights slightly, then more, and the audience fell silent. Dash looked out into the audience. All those open, expectant faces. He saw Houdini in the third row on the aisle—the seat that would have been Alex's in the Canon Theatre. His wheelchair was empty in the aisle.

And Sol Jacobson was in the seat beside him. His face was a mask. No expression at all, like he was asleep with his eyes open.

Herman Blumental stepped forward. Then Wolfgang appeared, dashing into a circle of light with a wand in his mouth. *Oh no, not the stupid squirrel.* Blumenthal leaned down to take the wand from his assistant's mouth. Dash had to admit Blumenthal was resplendent. As dazzling as a boney, messy-haired man could be, standing before them all in his borrowed suit. He even had a top hat. He took a bow. There were hoots and people applauded and beat their boots against the floor of the theatre. Wolfgang posed respectfully on Blumenthal's shoulder, facing forward, chittering at the audience.

"Welcome!" he called. "I am Blumenthal the Believer. And tonight, I have something very special to show to you. Miss Strauss, please?"

Miss Strauss?

It was the lady from backstage. Hannah. She was coming on from behind Dash, and she laid a hand on his shoulder as she went past. He saw Blumenthal beaming at her, and she suddenly skipped a little and ran toward him, carrying in one hand a metal ring about three feet in diameter.

Hannah held the ring up in the air. She turned it this way and that.

"What is this, this circle of life?" Blumenthal began, taking the ring from her. "Such a mystery . . . how we get here, what happens to us, why we find the people we find." He looked past the footlights at Houdini, who was still wearing his sunglasses.

"There are little *shapes* in the universe all around us," Blumenthal said. "Close up and far away! Inside, outside, under! It gets so a person doesn't know what way is up. But tonight . . . *tonight*, my friends . . . I will cast a light upon its dark mysteries!"

He winked and opened his right hand. A bolt of fire flew off his palm. The audience applauded for him. "For my big trick tonight, I propose we do the impossible!"

He clapped his hands twice and held them out. One went toward Hannah, the other toward Dash in the wings. Dash came onstage. They'd practised a little graceful entrance for him.

"Are you not going to take a volunteer?" came a voice from the audience.

It was Jacobson. He was standing. Houdini put his arm out to sit him down, but Jacobson shook him off. "I heard about what you're going to do tonight, and I object!"

"In what way, sir, do you object?" asked Blumenthal. He seemed surprised by Jacobson's interruption.

"You claim this will be the greatest trick ever performed. Other magicians have earned that mantle, sir. You have not. And you claim you can vanish this boy *without a trace*."

"Indeed, and that is what I intend to do."

"Then I have a challenge for you, oh great magician," said Jacobson. "I have brought a few friends along. Perhaps you will let them stand at all the exits—both to the theatre and the auditorium—to monitor all the wings and the backstage area, *and* below-stage as well?"

"The more the merrier!" said Blumenthal.

Dash tried to keep a straight face. Clearly, they had planned this. To ramp up the excitement. No one knew who Jacobson was, and not a soul in the place had any suspicion of who the little man in sunglasses was in the seat beside him.

"You are a doubter, are you?" said Blumenthal.

"Powerfully," said Jacobson.

"Well, if you insist, I have no choice. Bring in your men."

Jacobson clapped his hands twice and the rear doors of the auditorium flew open. A file of men in dark blue uniforms entered. Gluckman had raised the lights a little so people could see: they were policemen. Dash shot a look at Blumenthal, and he saw on the man's face that he had not been expecting Jacobson's friends to be the law. He carried on gamely.

"Well . . . Mr. Woolf, if you wouldn't mind—"

"Do you really think Harry Houdini would lend his name to

your pitiful cause?" snarled Jacobson. "You two charlatans? Go ahead and do your trick now. See if we don't find you out!"

Houdini was asking him to sit. The policemen went everywhere, into the wings, to the front of the audience, down the stairs that led to the traps beneath the stage.

Blumenthal gave Dash the ring, and he knew exactly where to put it. He looked up when he got to his spot. The fly space above appeared empty. The second ring wasn't up there. "Wolfgang?" the magician called. The squirrel had appeared again at the edge of the stage. The audience laughed nervously. They weren't sure what was going on.

Jacobson finally took his seat as Wolfgang leapt into their midst, causing a minor uproar, and finally, jumped up onto a rope that crossed overhead. One end was secured to the railing of the second balcony, the other vanished into the flies. In the middle of the rope was the second metal ring.

"If you wouldn't mind," said Blumenthal.

The squirrel ran down the rope and went to work on it with his teeth. Bits of frayed fibre drifted down into the audience. When the last strand broke, Wolfgang jumped onto the disk as it looped down toward the stage. Dash leapt back—it looked like the squirrel and ring might crash into the backdrop, but just as it came to the level of the stage, it suddenly straightened, like the rope had gone solid, and then it clacked down into place.

Blumenthal went over to it as the crowd broke into nervous applause. The magician nimbly untied the rope from the disk just as cables descended over the ring on the stage. He carried the ring to the cables and made a small show of attaching the cables to steel eyes distributed around the rim of the upper ring. The whole apparatus now rose and hovered about eight feet above the stage.

"If you will," said Blumenthal to Dash.

Dash stepped into the ring on the stage floor. Blumenthal walked away from him, to the front of the stage, and leaned into the dark where his audience sat. He spoke to them quietly, confidentially—Dash couldn't hear what he was saying. But he saw the hundreds of eyes gleaming in the dark beyond the magician, watching him intently, wanting to be amazed. Jacobson was sitting there with his arms crossed. But he was watching too.

The cops at the back of the auditorium locked the doors.

Walt, thought Dash.

The lights dimmed.

Blumenthal returned to his side. "Ready?" he whispered.

"Not really."

"But we go on anyway."

"If this doesn't work, we're both going to be in trouble."

"Then it had better work," said Blumenthal.

There was the whir of pulleys and the upper ring lowered again. It passed over Dash's head.

The magician intoned: "The line that divides life from death"—the upper ring clanked against the lower—"is as thin as the bubble that will now encase this young man."

There was a pause, and then the upper ring began to ascend again. A shimmering film of soap came up with it.

Dash lifted his eyes and saw sets of cables moving in different directions above him. Some all the way into the flies, some not as high. And . . . he was almost sure of it . . . there was a *third* ring as well.

"Hello?" said Blumenthal, interrupting his study. He was looking at Dash through the soap bubble.

"Sorry."

"As I was *saying*: only in magic can you disappear and . . . and then?"

It was cold now; the air felt like it was tightening around him. The bubble began to waver before his eyes.

"And then?" Blumenthal repeated.

"Come back," said Dashiel Woolf.

"Or not. Say so long, Dashiel."

Dash raised his hand in farewell. "So long," he said.

Herman Blumenthal had the pin in his hand now, a long hatpin, and the lights were getting brighter as he approached the bubble with its gleaming tip. Through the film, Dash could see Blumenthal's nervousness. The audience straining toward him. Houdini leaned forward in his seat, and at last he took off his sunglasses. As he stretched his head forward, an awful, sick feeling spread in Dash's chest and down to his stomach: it wasn't Houdini. It was Dmitri, his driver.

Houdini was still on the train to Detroit.

Sol Jacobson's mouth turned up slightly at the corners as bright ribbons of purple and green and yellow streaked across

Dash's vision. He saw the point of the hatpin coming through the bubble . . . and he heard Jacobson begin to laugh.

The light was unbearable. A rushing noise swarmed him. Something snapped, and then . . .

He was nowhere. A nowhere that was full of distant echoes and veins of darkness and . . .

Applause?

"But *wait*—!" came Herman Blumenthal's voice from somewhere nearby.

Dash's heart sank. He was still in 1926!

"—there's something else!"

Suddenly he wasn't floating in space anymore. He was moving, shifting. He was rising. Or he was falling. He wasn't sure anymore what was happening. There was a distinct clank and then a popping noise and just like that, he was standing on the stage in front of the audience. *Gluckman's* audience.

So he *was* going to be stuck here forever!

The applause went on. The men in cloth caps stood, and the women in their sad dresses stood, and even the children were standing on the seats, and they were all applauding. Jacobson remained seated and Dash saw his lips part in disbelief. There was a flicker of movement to his right and he looked over: a line of men was ascending the steps to the stage. They were dressed identically: black overcoats and black hats, but they were all different ages. The one in front looked like a teenager, but the one behind was older. And the one behind him was the man who'd helped him get onto the streetcar when he first arrived, and the man behind *him* was the one who'd saved him from Constable Montrose. At the end, the man with the walrus moustache came up the stairs on a cane. They all wore black rings on their lapels: the ring Walt had given them as a gift, when they were just boys, eleven-year-old boys, having the adventure of their lives.

They marched toward him one by one, vanishing just as they came to the edge of the ring in which he stood.

His somehow future selves.

Some of the policemen were now rushing back into the auditorium with perplexed looks on their faces. Three of them ran out of the wings, right past him, as if he weren't there at all. Dmitri was applauding madly.

The whole audience had taken to its feet, and Dash saw other shapes now, other bodies: a second phantasmal audience appearing overtop of the fading Pantages crowd. Behind their standing ovation were men and woman sitting in the seats, ghosts in ties taking pictures with their phones, ladies in loud print dresses, kids in T-shirts. And they were applauding as well. Slowly, they melted through the audience of 1926, their forms joining, both audiences applauding in raucous delight.

Blumenthal swept his arm down again, bending at the waist and drinking in the adulation. But when he stood, his thin, bony shoulders began to thicken and a wave of white hair unfurled down the back of his head. His borrowed suit began to shine. He swept his top hat, blackly gleaming in the lights, toward Dash, and he was Bloom, Bloom the Beguiler, and Herman Blumenthal's audience fluttered like candle flame guttering, and grew faint. So faint.

And then they were gone.

"Let's hear it for my young assistant," Bloom cried.

Dash realized he could step out of the ring. He came forward onstage and the applause continued. He saw his parents in the third row, smiling grandly. The lights came up in the theatre and here he was, it was over, and the doors were opening at the back of the auditorium. Dash could feel the modern air coming down the aisles.

27

He clung to his parents as everyone filed out of the theatre. His mother had him tucked up tight beside her and his dad was talking to people who had gathered in a small knot alongside them.

"Well, unfortunately, he came back," he said, smiling down at Dash. "Not much to do about that!"

People laughed.

"How long was I gone for?" Dash asked him.

"Oh gosh, it was so peaceful it felt like it went on forever!"

People were jostling in. "Was it scary?" a young boy asked him. "Where did you go when you weren't on the stage?"

"Oh, I can't tell you *that*," he said. "It would ruin the trick."

"But I want to know," the boy said.

"Do tell!" came the voice of a woman behind them. "Tell us all! Did you go under the stage?"

He looked around for the kid who'd given him the envelope, but he was nowhere to be seen.

"Well, it's very interesting," said Dash. "I went back in time and tried to save Harry Houdini's life."

There was appreciative laughter.

"How did it go?" said someone else.

"I failed," said Dash.

Home. He'd never think of the word, or the place, the same way again.

He slouched in the back seat of the car as his father drove, staring up through the window at the now-clear nighttime sky, a sky fringed by the city's light.

His mother turned in the passenger seat. "Did you enjoy that?" she asked him.

"Yes . . . thank you," he said. "It was a wonderful . . . night."

The car trundled east, toward Greektown. They hadn't called it that in 1926. It had been just Danforth Avenue. He had no idea when all the Greek people and the Greek food arrived. Tomorrow he was going to ask his dad to get him a Greek salad, one full of every colour under the sun, with feta cheese and olives, and he wanted a Coke with sugar in it and a box of Oreos.

"Look how tired he is," his mother said.

As they walked up to the house, he reached for his father's key. "I want to do it," he said.

He unlocked the door and swung it open. That smell. The fridge humming in the dark.

He raced upstairs, saw the cabinet with the glass door right beside the bathroom, as it always had been, the towels folded in it. A picture of him at age seven, crouching inside a hockey net, hung on the wall in the hallway. Then there was the picture of all three of them, a professional portrait of them standing under a tree. He could still recall the feel of the itchy sweater he'd had to wear.

His bedroom looked just as he'd left it earlier that evening. Schoolbooks tossed on the desk, the clothes he'd been wearing on the floor. Two rejected ties on the bed. Good thing he'd had that suit jacket.

And there was his bed, under the window. His bookshelf. The hoop on the back of his closet door. It was his room in his house where he lived with his parents, Holly and David Woolf.

His mum helped him off with his suit and hung it up for him. She noticed the bruise on his calf, and touched it lightly. The mark the rail bull's truncheon had left on him. He told her someone had whacked him in stickball. It hurt when she touched it: the pain had come back with him.

He brushed his teeth with real toothpaste. Everyone was exhausted. It was nice when the day ended and the house shut down, he thought. There was a peaceful togetherness in it.

Dash snapped off his light and got under his covers. Then he got out and turned the light back on. He pulled the bed away from the wall and looked down into the crack. It was too dark to see the floor. He felt around with his fingertip, searching for a shape. The floor had probably been re-stained a dozen times in eighty-five years.

"Everything okay?" asked his father from the hallway.

"I dropped something."

"It'll still be there in the morning, Captain Vanish."

"You're right," he said, but then he felt something against his fingernail. A straight indent, about a centimetre long. And a big curving line connecting the top of it to the bottom. A capital *D*.

"Come on now, Dash."

He flopped back into the bed, holding his face still. "Sorry."

His father switched off the light and Dash got back under his covers.

"Fun tonight, wasn't it?"

"It was," said Dash. "Long night . . ."

"Went by like a flash for me. Hey," he said, coming in to pull Dash's covers up. "When did you get your hair cut?"

"Uh . . . last week. You didn't notice?"

"I must be on another planet these days."

Nothing like the one I've been on, Dash thought.

He went out past his mum, who was leaning against his door frame, a silhouette. She came in to say good night too.

"You know, sweetie?"

"Yes?"

"Mrs. Singh wrote to me. She says Alex has written you six emails, but you never answered. Why don't you reply?"

He felt too ashamed of himself to answer her.

"Will you please write to him? He obviously misses you and it's unkind not to reply. Don't you think?"

"Yes," he said. "It is."

She leaned down to kiss him, blocking the light with her warmth. "You will learn that there are many ways to have a friendship, Dashiel. If distance alone kills it, it wasn't a friendship in the first place. He's your friend. You should honour that."

"I will. I'll write to him."

"Good. Oh, I found something in your suit pocket." She took an envelope out of her bathrobe pocket. "Who is this from?"

"That . . . OH!" he said.

"What?"

TOMORROW. The card said *tomorrow*. Not 1926. *Today's* tomorrow. His heart suddenly flailed around in his chest. *Walt*.

"Dash?"

"It's an invitation," he said in an unnaturally high voice. "An invitation. From a friend. He's inviting me to a party after school tomorrow!"

"Well, that's wonderful! You should go."

"Can I?"

"I'm thrilled that you want to. Of course. Good night, sweetheart. I love you."

28

Dreamlessness. He'd earned it. He had travelled down so deep into darkness and nothingness that when he opened his eyes, he wondered if he'd slept at all. But when he woke up, it was morning, and he was in the world he came from, the only one he really knew.

He got up and got dressed. Jeans, T-shirt, ankle socks. He took his phone and his keys. He felt in the pockets of his good suit. There were still some coins in there, including a quarter dated *1924*. His mum had left the small, white envelope on his dresser.

Walking around in his bedroom, it was almost exactly like yesterday morning, which was either twenty-four hours or six days ago. But it felt now that the roof of his house was missing and he was walking around on a stage in front of an invisible audience. Maybe the audience was only himself. Or maybe it was everyone and everything, always.

*

Dash poured himself a huge bowl of Count Chocula and drowned it in milk. His parents leaned against the kitchen counter, drinking their coffees, watching him.

"Did you go for a twelve-mile jog in the middle of the night?" his dad asked.

"I'm hungry."

"That's a lot of cereal."

"Look at him," said his mother. "He's like four pieces of linguini stuck to a carrot. Let him eat."

"Yeah, let him eat," said Dash, slopping milk into the bowl.

"At least don't put so much into your mouth at once," said his dad.

His mother held her hand out for his bowl. "Hey, Dash got invited to a party! After school today."

"Frantabulous," said his father. "Need a lift?"

"It's okay," said Dash. "It's in the neighbourhood."

"Then back for dinner by six," his mum said. "You have hockey. Or is your friend's mum doing dinner? I suppose you could skip your—" She spun a look to his dad. "We could see a movie."

"I don't think it's dinner," said Dash.

"Oh. Well, then, be home by six, sweetie."

After his breakfast, his dad gave him his lunchbox and Dash slipped it into his knapsack. He snuck a safety pin off his mother's dresser. They both kissed him out the door.

He walked to the bus stop. Victor Avenue. On November 1, 2011. Too unreal. Too real.

Mr. Leonidis was picking leaves off his lawn one by one. "Heh, Dashy!" he called, waving.

"Hi, Mr. Leonidis," he said, waving back.

"Good boy, eh?"

He got onto his school bus and went to school, and it was a Tuesday like any other Tuesday, especially in the way he couldn't wait for it to be over. But today, the reason was very different.

French, gym, recess, lunch, math, home economics, English. As the day went by, occasionally he felt that he was a part of it. Most of the time, he didn't.

Somehow, three o'clock finally rolled around. Then he was free and there was electricity in his veins. He used the safety pin to attach the black ring to the front of his jacket. Arundel Avenue was only a five-minute walk, and he'd been invited for four o'clock, but he couldn't wait. He had to go right away.

It was the same house, but it seemed so much more alive now. The front yard was a patch of fading green, and rose bushes under the window still held a few of their leaves. The steps were painted blue and all the curtains were open.

A small Canadian flag hung from a rod on one of the painted columns that framed the steps. He climbed them as quietly as he could, his breath tight, and went up to the door. Through one of the windows in the front he saw a room full of books.

He knocked. A few seconds passed and then he heard footsteps from inside. No big, mustachioed face appeared in the window, but the door opened a few inches, and then all the way—and there, standing on the threshold, was the boy he'd seen backstage. The same boy, with the same dark-brown hair and clear blue eyes.

"You're early," he said. "He's here!" he called down the hall.

A voice came from deep inside the house. It said, "Well, let him in, then."

Dash stepped tentatively into the hallway. It led back into the main floor of the house. It wasn't made of apartments anymore. Some of the walls he'd seen were gone now. It was brighter and more open.

"Take your shoes off," said the boy.

Dash did, and the boy brought him into the kitchen, which looked out onto the garden beyond. An old woman in a light blue dress was sitting at the table.

"I've only just put the pie in to heat!" she said. She picked up her glasses off the table and put them on. "It really is you," she said.

Dash looked behind him into the living room, but it was empty. An old typewriter sat on a table. "Who are you?" he asked.

"People call me Wendy now. But you know me as Dee Dee."

Dash pulled out a chair from the table and slowly lowered himself into it. "Dee Dee?" She took her glasses off again and he saw her blue eyes. Like the boy's. Like Walter's. "Dee Dee," he said under his breath. "*Oh no . . .*"

"It's all right—"

"The card was from you? Where's Walter?"

"Oh, pet" was all she said, and Dashiel put his head down on his arms. He heard the boy shuffle out of the room.

"He died a long time ago," said Dee Dee.

"I thought he was going to be here!"

"I'm sorry. He passed twenty-one years ago. At eighty-five."

He lifted his head. "I can't believe it. I was just with him."

"I know. And I was so hoping you would come and tell us all about it. I've waited so long to see you again."

"But—"

"I know. It must seem very odd to you. You've been through a lot in such a short time. But you have to understand: this is a wonderful day for me. I've waited my whole life for this day." She rose from the table. "Come and sit."

He followed her into the living room, and sat quietly in a chair. Her house was comfortable, with soft, yellow light. But there was a hollow feeling in his belly.

Dee Dee brought out lemonade she'd had chilling in the fridge and poured him a glass, but he couldn't touch it. She moved a ball of yarn off a chair and sat.

"He had a wonderful life," she said. "He had children, and grandchildren. And then he got old and he died. He would have loved to see you again."

"I thought . . ."

"Sometimes," she continued softly, "when we were younger, you were all he could talk about. He told me everything that happened. More than once, in fact. Although, I forget some of it now. He would always say you'd escaped without paying him back his quarter!"

"I brought it to give to him."

She made a sad face. "What a dear boy you are. Oh, bless." She leaned forward and pushed herself up. "I'm burning that pie."

"I don't really want—"

"Of course you do," she said, waving her hand at him. "It's quince."

She returned to the kitchen and he waited in the living room feeling empty. Walter was dead. Dead! He wanted to cry.

She returned with three plates. "My mother had made a quince pie that day, if I'm remembering correctly. I hope I am."

"She did," said Dash. "I was starving."

"And I had a little cold. I was only six. You entertained me."

"Yes." He put his head down again to shield his eyes.

"Oh dear," she said, and passed him a napkin.

"Did you believe him?" asked Dash, accepting a plate and a fork. "About me?"

"I did. He never told the story differently. And Walter, you know, he wasn't the most imaginative kid on the block. He was made for other things. When we were older, he didn't talk about it much, but nearer the end . . . the memories came back. He remembered you as if it were yesterday. It made him happy, to feel you near. He left me that envelope in his will. Told me to make sure it got to the right seat, on Halloween 2011. I added the note, of course."

He sank his fork into the tender crust. The first taste was like getting into a time machine again. "That's the same pie."

"I still have her recipe."

He saw how it made her happy to watch him eat. Dee Dee. That little girl.

"He left you something else, Dash."

He lowered the fork. "What?"

"Herman Blumenthal performed the trick only the once, you know."

"I know."

"He never took it out of its crate again. Wouldn't perform it, and people offered him good money too. When he died, Walter got a letter. Blumenthal had left him the trick." Dash's fork clinked onto his plate. "And Walter kept it safe. For Joseph Bloom. And for you."

A wide smile spread across his face.

"It's yours now."

"It's *mine*?"

"When you turn eighteen, yes."

His thunderstruck expression made Dee Dee laugh. "So maybe you *will* see Walter again."

Yes, he would. He touched the ring on his jacket.

"Ah," said Dee Dee, looking past him. The boy had come into the room. "This is my great-grand-nephew. Named for his great-grandfather. There are three Walter Gibsons now, I must tell you."

Dash laughed. "That's too many."

"Hey!" Walter Gibson narrowed his eyes. "Good thing you had at least one, from the sound of it."

"So you know?"

"Know what?" growled Walter. He remained at the edge of the room with his fists balled against his hips. "That you went back in time?" He snorted. "Yeah, and I'm Elvis."

"Come in and sit down, young man," said Dee Dee. "There's no need to be rude."

The boy entered, glowering. Dash offered his hand. "Dashiel Woolf," he said.

"Whatever," said the boy, but he shook Dash's hand.

Dee Dee passed him a plate of pie. "He met your great-grandfather, you know. He remembers him better than I do."

"She's been telling this story since I was four," the boy muttered.

"I did know your great-grandfather," Dash said quietly. "When he was eleven. You look just like him. You even talk like him. And he would half-close his left eye—like you're doing right now—when he didn't believe what he was hearing. Which was often, at first."

Walter Gibson looked away. "You really knew him?" he asked.

"I saw him last night. And you know what?"

The other boy ran a fingernail between his front teeth.

"Walter?"

Walter looked back. "What?"

"I owe him twenty-five cents. I was going to pay him back

if he was here . . ." He took out the 1924 quarter and offered it to him. "Can I give it to you?"

Walter glanced at the quarter and then up at his great-grand-aunt. She nodded to him, and he reached forward and took it from Dash.

"That means my debt is paid," Dash said.

"You think so?" said Dee Dee, smiling mischievously. "I don't see any quarter." She lifted her chin toward Walter, who held the coin in the flat of his palm.

"Keep your eye on it," he said.

Dash watched him wave his hand back and forth slowly over the coin.

"Once," said Walter Gibson, grinning. "Twice . . ."

Author's Notes

A Note to Readers

The lecture Harry Houdini gives in this novel happened on October 19, 1926, in the afternoon, at McGill University in Montreal. For the purposes of this story, I have changed that date to October 20, 1926. The characters of Sol Jacobson and Jacques Pelletier are fictional. Houdini had an English agent named Harry Day with whom he was close, but Day didn't accompany him on tour. Finally, it is unlikely that Houdini performed the Water Torture Cell in his performance of October 22 owing to the fact that he'd injured his ankle in Albany, New York, earlier in the month.

Two of Houdini's speeches in this novel are taken from real life: much of his speech to the lecture audience at McGill, and his stage pattern for the Water Torture Cell.

A Note to Magicians

I'm not absolutely sure how to do the Soap Bubble Vanish. My theory about how it *could* be done is reflected in little textual clues in the various discussions about and depictions of the trick. But I'm not talking.

Still, I'd love to see it.

How about it, magicians?

A Note to Time Travellers
If I'm wrong about any of this, please let me know.

MR
February 2, 2014

Acknowledgments

My thanks first and foremost to Hadley Dyer, who cajoled and jollied me until I wrote a novel for young adults, and I'm grateful to her for her persistence as well as her marvellous editorial eye. At HarperCollins, my gratitude as well to Maria Golikova and Allyson Latta.

Thank you to my long-time friend and agent, Ellen Levine.

Especial thanks to the following, all young readers who volunteered to read an earlier draft of this novel and who responded to it with verve, excitement, and many valuable comments: Karim Alatrash, Adam and Oliver Bock, Abigail Cooper, Max Friedman-Cole, Beatrice Freedman, Gemma Fudge, Katharine Galloway, Frances and Edward Hayward, Nico Heer, Henry Morrison, Michael O'Regan, and Summer Singh. Thanks also to the mums and dads who volunteered their kids and who, in many cases, read the draft themselves and were generous with their comments.

IF YOU LOVED THIS BOOK YOU'LL ALSO WANT TO READ:

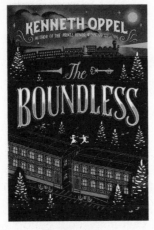

The Boundless
by Kenneth Oppel

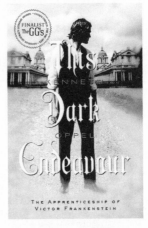

The Apprenticeship
of Victor Frankenstein series
by Kenneth Oppel

All the Wrong Questions series
by Lemony Snicket

The Hunchback
Assignments series
by Arthur Slade

*The Graverobber's
Apprentice*
by Allan Stratton

FOR TEACHING RESOURCES AND MORE VISIT
♥HarperClassroom.ca